THE
MOORISH
WHORE

THE
MOORISH
WHORE

A NOVEL

REBEKAH SCOTT

To Filipe Branco Madeira, a character's best friend

ACKNOWLEDGMENT

Debt is owed to the kindly Madres Benedictinas of Holy Cross Monastery, Sahagún, Leon, Spain, where I first met Zaida the Moor. Poetry cited here is adapted from "The Poems of Mu'tamid, King of Seville," translated from Arabic by Dulcie Lawrence Smith and published in 1915, now distributed by Antioch Gate, Oxford UK. Used with permission.

BEGINNING

Once I was a princess, a Moorish princess, a Muslim, daughter of Mu´tamid the wily poet-king of Seville. My name was Zaida. I was raised in a palace, dressed in silks, taught to read and count, and schooled in sensuality. My father promised me to the Emir of Denia, but I was ruined by the Grand Vizier, my father's faithless friend.

Alfonso the Christian king of Leon and Castilla carried me off as a prize of war. He hauled me home the way his soldiers carried away the Moors' sheep and cows. The army took us all back to the byres in the north for breeding. It was there I was given a new Christian name, Isabel. I was married in the Christian church, but because of my "impure blood" I was not accorded the rights of the wife of a king. I was "the king's concubine." Or sometimes, "that Moorish whore."

The king had outlived his second wife, the religious one who brought the black-robed monks with her when she came to Castilla y Leon from Cluny, in France. I was a

Moorish girl, practically African, with dark eyes and skin and the long legs and veils. I was utterly different from the pious, pale queens who came before me. I laughed and danced, recited exotic poems of faraway souks and almond trees. I warmed the blood of the aging king, acted on his desires, and eventually gave him a son.

Alfonso, as was only fitting, had me baptized and cat-echized the faith of Jesus Christ. For four years I kept him occupied while the monks looked round France for a more fitting, fair-skinned and Christian queen.

I could have been a princess or even a queen in Toledo, Alfonso's newest, most cosmopolitan conquest. But instead the king settled me on the plain in the north in San Facund, a town he'd given over to the black-robed priests from France. It was the worst possible place for a dark-skinned daughter of Muhammad. I was disliked at the monastery and parts of the town, looked upon as a pagan, a prostitute, or even something less than human. The king was rarely with me there, but I managed to give him three children.

I died whilst giving birth to the king's only son. I never was queen in Castile, but the king made sure my body was laid in a place of honor near the altar in the monastery of San Facundo. Much as he enjoyed me while I lived, he did not mourn for long when I died.

That is what history says. Like most of history, only parts of it are true.

I am very much alive. I am setting down the truth of my life, even if it is unwelcome or inconvenient to some. My story forms part of the heritage of our kings and rulers, so it should be written. Truth must be set down, says Father José Diego Mondragon, confessor to this foundation.

I am a professed nun, cloistered, hidden from sight. My health is not good, the climate here is damp and cold, and my story is a long. I pray I can finish this work before time finishes me.

Building begins soon on our chapter house. Father José Diego will seal this story with several more founding documents into the great stones, where it can stay until all of the people described here are dust, forgotten, history. I also enclose the letters and documents that prove its truth.

+ *Sr. Mary Isabel*
Princess Isabel of Denia,
Zaida bint Mu'tamid

Autumn AD 1110

I

THE SOUND OF MOVING WATER

Jasmine scented my first sixteen years in this world. I was Zaida, firstborn daughter of the brilliant court of Mu´tamid of Sevilla, in the west of the great kingdom that was Al Andaluz. I lived in a white palace. Sunlight shone off the tiled walls, the air was full of perfume, and the beautiful, wide River Guadalquivir flowed outside the windows. Hillsides bloomed with palms and almond trees. My father was the king, my parents were lovers, and Sevilla in those days was legendary, full of music, poetry, and the sound of moving water.

The novices love to hear me describe it. It's as if I have my own canon of Scripture stories, and these mountain girls are keen to memorize each detail.

"Tell us about the flowers. Tell us about the ants, the almond blossoms like snow," they sing out to me on afternoons when we are free to speak. "Sing us a song, the ones your father wrote!"

It is from telling all those stories, reciting all those poems, I can easily write them now. They are fresh in my
mind, worn smooth from much recalling.

The Moors, my people, pray five times each day, and
before their prayers they wash: head, hands, feet at least.
Each neighborhood is home to a hammam, a bath-house,
so even the most common folk can enjoy a good scrub in
clean water each week. Our palace had three hammams,
with hot, warm, and cool pools, rose petals, warm oil...
How I longed for a hammam once I moved to the north! I
brought the washing habit with me, if not the prayers; I cut
my demand for clean, hot water to once each day. It drove
the servants mad at first, especially on the road.

When I was shown my rooms in the royal apartments of
the Monastery of San Facund, I was given clothing worn by
Ines and Constanza, the dead queens who preceded me—
thick brocade gowns, layers of wool, wimples and turbans
of fine thick cloth, even some lovely lace. None of it had
been properly washed. (Poor Ines had died wearing one of
the shifts!) They had been put away damp, in a cupboard
crawling with vermin.

I opened all the windows and had all the hangings taken
down and beaten. The floors were scrubbed, the rushes re-
placed. I sent my new wardrobe to the river and every scrap
was washed. I had to wear the dresses I had traveled in
while the heavy clothes dried. Their wet-wool stink filled
the house, the damp linen itched and galled my skin. But I
no longer smelled the skin of dead women against my own.

My cleanliness cost the household endless toil, but
what is a princess for if not maintaining? I asked to have a
fountain installed in the cloister, a watering-trough in the

stables, and moving water supplies in the king's rooms and mine—and the abbot's. It was shocking and outlandish. But with me from Sevilla my father had sent Hamid ibn Khalikan, a man adept in the arts of water, air, and buildings. (I shall write more about him!) After a period of digging and shouting, the sweet sound of falling water and birdsong filled the courtyard.

The water had its effect. Songbirds inhabited the cloister. The abbot noticed when the skin of his wrists stopped staining his sleeves black. He praised the Holy Virgin for healing the terrible rash that had afflicted him for years.

People in the north do not understand the flow of air and water. Their houses, even the nobles' houses, are damp halfway up the walls, spotted dark. They stink of smoke and grease. The windows are tiny holes in thick walls. The streets are too narrow even for carts to pass, and the donkeys, horses, dogs, and swine leave the lanes steaming with dung and piss, ankle-deep in flies and mud. It is not so much in the southern cities, where the elements are kinder, and bend to the will and the wisdom of trained men.

In Sevilla the main streets were wide and straight, paved, with channels to carry away the muck. Animals were not left to wander. Our streets smelled of rain and intrigue. But San Facund was a stinking place, and cold as hell in winter. Wind blew straight off the little River Cea, through the hallway casements and under the doors. It blew down the chimneys and put out the lights, and filled my rooms with smoke.

In a little ivory casket I kept a handful of jasmine flowers I plucked off the vine as I walked my last round of the garden at my father's palace, on my way out the gate. They were white and tender. I kept that casket near me through those first smoky winters, and I still keep it near me here. Twenty years on, the flowers are crumbling to dust. They are great treasures, because they've held their beautiful perfume. I only need to open the lid and their scent sends me back to the blue-and-white tiled garden with its shimmering fountain in the center.

I wish I had broken off a branch, or somehow learned the secret of starting jasmine vines. I asked the king to have one planted in the courtyard, but he told me jasmine cannot survive so far north. The gardeners at the monastery had no knowledge of the plant. I still sometimes wish for jasmines in this cloister, to fill our garden with their scent, and send it over the wall and into the fields outside. I wonder if it would carry so far. I wonder if anyone would notice.

In San Facund the dirt, the smells and the cold were the most difficult things for me at first. I was a spoiled girl with an over-sensitive nose. I did not know I was living at the center of Christian Iberia, in the finest apartments of the finest cloister in the land. I was not very grateful.

It was not all bad. Instead of warbling muezzins calling us to pray from minarets, we had bells to ring out the hours from the monastery tower. I loved the singing in the cloister and the choir, and the sing-song of the vendors in the street, and the thunder of the hooves of hundreds of sheep being driven through the city gate and up to the market square. Sometimes I heard the pilgrims singing in their monastery wing, playing strange music on flutes and pipes.

In San Facund there was music, but no poetry. Once in a while a passing jongleur would entertain us with hero-stories, but most of what we heard were Psalms, chanted in the saddest keys, set for mourning, not dancing. That is sad, because I came to love the Psalms of David and Solomon. It is the holy scripture I learned first, and still know best. They are full of joy, but are sung so sadly I wonder if the singers know the words they chant.

But San Facund was my home, the place where my husband the king chose to send me. I do not criticize, for I know now what a privileged life I had there, so much better than most other women could imagine. I lived in beautiful rooms with beamed ceilings, and slept on a bed of wool and linen and goose-down. In winter I wore heavy cloth from Gascony and Bordeaux, and thick tapestry hung on my walls to hide the cold stones. A fire burned in the grate to keep me warm the year round.

When the king was with me, I was warm indeed, cosseted and entertained. But my king was a warrior, with a huge country to manage. His visits were far apart, and never lasted long enough.

Alfonso is a great fighter, an impatient negotiator, and a violent man. Among my people—his enemies—the Moors, he is feared and respected, because unlike so many soldiers he keeps his word and honors his treaties. He is pious and superstitious, he does not lie well or easily. (I write assuming he is still in this world. If he lives he must be quite old now.) I learned early that girlish manipulation annoyed him, that I could simply ask for what I wanted and he would give it to me.

He was not a man to be manipulated. The monks were the only people who did that successfully.

Alfonso loved his Burgundian monks, and was in awe of French things and people. I wondered for a while if the monks bewitched him, until I learned the monks thought I was a witch!

I was a new Christian, looked-on with suspicion. My skin was dark (it still is dark), I prayed like an infidel still sometimes, calling God "most merciful," I was tolerated in their midst only because the king brought me there—the same king who gave the monastery its vast riches and rights and powers. The abbot himself was spectacularly powerful, practically a prince himself, but he could not afford to defy the king.

Like any kingdom, Castilla y Leon is full of ancient feuds and double-dealing. It is not so different from Sevilla on that account—this is why I took an interest. Often in the night, when we finished with our lovemaking, the king and I talked long about the business of war and politics. He believed I could not grasp such manly subjects. But women are born politicians, we are supreme diplomats. Where men simply draw swords or bows to slay and enslave, our language is negotiation and seduction.

Alfonso indulged me. I was exotic, different from most women he knew, and I was always pleasing to him: Clean, smiling, and present. The king desired me because I smelled good. And because I loved to be touched. And because sometimes I touched him first. I loved my husband, and I believed him when he said he loved me. He was not only a king, and I was not just a whore who thought herself a queen. We were lovers, at least for a while. We bound ourselves to one another, for hours at a time, for weeks and months.

I think of those times, and I must stop myself from slipping into the sin of lust. Even at my age, my body still is moved by the thought of his great, hard hands grasping my hips or ankles, or the feel of his bristly face on the skin of my neck. How wondrous it was to see him respond to a sideways glance, to see him gaze at me. From across the pews in the chapel, from the backs of our horses while riding out to hunt, from the floor of our overheated chamber, the king and I delighted one another.

The monks made it clear we were too noisy together, unseemly and beastly. And as nature dictates, all that coupling meant I was always with child by the time the king rode away from San Facund. Much as they said they wanted a male heir for the throne, the monks did not want it to come with the taint of Moorish blood.

In the months when Alfonso was away, I lived the advice of my mother. I was the sea bird that floats along the top of the waves. She keeps her place, letting the motion move under and around her, but feeling little or nothing of the storm. And so for four years I floated on the grey water of San Facund, pretending not to notice the sneers and slights.

Like a gull on the waves, or a mare in a good stable with fresh straw, I did not consider the future. I had a pretty face and a singing voice, and a young body that responded to desire and produced children. That was enough for the king in those days. And as long as the king cared for me, my enemies dared not harm me.

I will write more fluidly as time passes and I become accustomed. Please practice patience with me. I am old, and this style of writing is not familiar to me.

2
Hamid: A Plumb-Line

Hamid Ibn Khalikan was short and bow-legged. He was near-sighted, and squinted and frowned and held things close to his face to better see them. He was baptized a Christian alongside me, but I am sure he still bows to the east at least once a day, if he lives. He is brilliant, a man of God.

I mentioned Hamid yesterday, as the engineer who made the water move through the royal apartments of the monastery of San Facundo. My mind stayed on him through the night, and I prayed for his soul, and the souls of his family. They were truly my family in San Facund, the truest Christians I have met, even if they are Moors. I pray all of God's blessings upon him.

It is clear to me now that Hamid was a spy, sent north with me by my forever-scheming father. Hamid could read and write in Arabic as well as Romance, and messages traveled north and south along with his shipments of terra-cotta pipes and tiles. It was from Hamid I learned of events in

Sevilla. When the rest of the world conspired to keep me in darkness, Hamid gave me the light of truth and friendship.

While wars and politics provide a dull background to most of the lives around us, ours were lived at times in a strange mirror. Good news for Christian Leon and Castilla often meant something else for us. One late summer morning, soon before my Elvira was born, bells pealed in the churches and the people cheered the latest news from the front in Granada—King Alfonso's army was victorious! I went into the garden to collect flower petals, to throw out my window and into the street for the celebration.

Hamid was there, pretending to adjust the flow into the watering trough. He turned to me, grave. He handed me a cake of pressed figs, a treat from the far south. "Zaida, sad news," he said. "The king won the battle. But your brother Muhammad was there, fighting. He was killed."

Hamid could not touch me, or offer any kind of comfort. I ran, trying not to cry out until I was safely alone in my room. While San Facund celebrated the faraway victory, I cried for my lost brother. And for hours, down below in the garden, Hamid stood by.

For as long as I knew him, he called me Zaida.

He was a man, and a Moor, but permitted to speak or write to me occasionally as he was considered a part of my retinue. We helped one another. In commissioning the fountains and troughs in the royal apartments of the monastery, I gave Hamid opportunity to demonstrate his skills to the most powerful people in the district. Soon every rich man wanted a water supply in his yard, and pipes to drain away the damp. In time Hamid took on apprentices, some of them sons of old Christian families.

His labor was hard and long. Uncultivated earth in San Facundo is unyeilding clay, difficult to dig and impossible to drain. Hamid complained of bad tools and surly laborers—even when he showed them a more efficient way to dig ditches, they instantly returned to their wasteful, laborious techniques. Hamid used tools familiar in the south: compass and plumb lines and angles. One of the laborers reported him to the abbot, saying he was a wizard!

Hamid was duly summoned to give account and demonstrate these wonders. It was a damp morning, but the cloister was packed with fascinated citizens. I had a perfect view from my window, and held my baby up so she could see, too. Hamid stood below me, atop a mounting block, and dug into the pouch of tools slung over his shoulder. Out came a length of twine with a tiny bit of lead tied to one end.

"This, your graces, is a plumb line," he said to them, in perfect courtesy. He held the line halfway up its length, and let the bob fall ground-ward. "No matter the condition of rain, temperature, or season, this line shall hang perfectly upright, straight and true. Even if I stand askew," he said, leaning at a crazy angle with his body, making a little rhyme with his words, "The line is perfectly upright. And a wall, or this mounting block," he said, aligning the bob to his perch, "may appear to your eye to be upright and true, this little line will reveal the truth to you." The block was cut at a gentle angle, not visible to the casual glance. The little string showed where the mason had taken liberties. The gathered crowd sighed to itself, then cried out: Put it against this wall, this column, the door here! Let me try!

Hamid demonstrated several of the tools in the bag, explaining the uses of each in simplest terms: angles. A compass, a chalking-line. He credited the Greeks, the Romans, Medes and Persians. He did not show them all his tools—but they did not know that.

Many of the people had never seen such things, but his simple approach removed the mystery. The forge was kept busy for the following months making crude copies, and perhaps the walls and curbs of San Facund were made more straight from then on. (It was at that moment I too first learned how these tools applied to building. I was until then as ignorant as any cowherd where engineering is concerned. The knowledge I gained there has served me well in recent years.)

None of Hamid's sewer-lines and water-works could compare to the watered orangeries of Cordoba, but they were revelations to the simple people of San Facund. When something he built was seen to function—a grindstone powered by a water wheel, a submerged pump, an irrigated terrace—they marveled as if it was sent from God.

In the fullness of time, Hamid was put to work widening and draining the boggy streets, straightening and even paving some of them. The king and the abbot decided that San Facund must have a straight, paved avenue, like a true city—parallel to the river, along the front of the abbey, and public fountains at the springs to serve the neighborhoods and the pilgrim hostel. Hamid made use of pipes and waterways dug hundreds of years ago by the Romans, brilliant men who founded San Facund—what remained of them after centuries of looting. (San Facund is a city without stone. The place is made of mud and sticks. Even the finest buildings cannot last for long. Hamid forever wished for stones, and made do with bricks.)

Hamid made many enemies. He was hated by those whose buildings, built too near the curbs, had to be cut back or torn down. When he proved the tanner's stinking pools were poisoning the water supply in the Jewish quarter, a nighttime visitor splashed a bucket of overripe urine across the doorstep of Hamid's house. A convert Moor was an easy target for people powerless to defy the abbot or king, those commissioning the works.

Hamid paid his bills and his workers on time, and the fruits of his labor were easily seen in the streets and plazas of the town. He made many more friends than enemies. One was Olaya, the pretty widow of a Moorish cattle dealer. She had three sons, a ready smile, and a farmyard in dire need of drainage.

Hamid was delighted at one aspect of life in San Facund: women were much more visible there than they were in Al-Andaluz. The wives and daughters of cattle dealers and potters and farmers did not often have servants to fetch water for them—they washed their own linen out in the sunshine on the riverbank alongside the Jewesses and the Christian girls. They bought and sold at the market, they could speak freely with men, up to a point. Some of them made their own decisions.

Olaya was one of those. She ran her husband's business with a steady hand, but with her feeble-minded brother Ali as her representative—otherwise she would be paid half the going price for her animals, and taxed twice as much, as is common everywhere in the world.

When Hamid Ibn Khalikan expressed his interest, Olaya gladly accepted his suit. Her cattle-yard soon became a neat barn and paddock, and her tumbledown house stood up straight and tall at the corner where the Moorish Quarter meets the cemetery. Hamid coated the mud bricks with a substance that protects them from rain, so Olaya need not cover them again each year with mud and straw. To celebrate their wedding, he painted the whole a remarkable bright ochre.

I fear the passage of time in those days has left my memory in a muddle. The king was away, fighting Moors in the south and Galicians in the west, signing accords in Toledo and Gascony. He returned to San Facund in winter, and often the court came down as well, to escape the worst of the mountain snows of Leon. I did not appear at the court, but in those days I saw more of the king than anyone else. He spent his days with them, and his nights with me.

It was only fitting, especially for a ruler. My grandfather, King al-Mu'Tadid, was a poet as well as my father. He wrote a verse on the very topic, and Alfonso learned it by heart and recited it back to his dukes and counts when excusing himself one the evening:

> I divide my time between hard work and leisure,
> Mornings for affairs of state, evenings for pleasure!
> At night I indulge in amusements and frolics,
> At noon I rule with a proud mein in my court;
> Amidst my trysts I do not neglect my striving
> For glory and fame;
> these I always plan to attain.

(In Arabic, I assure you, it rhymes quite neatly!)

They thought it funny, a Christian king reciting heathen poems. They had no poems of their own to offer, not even a witty rejoinder. Alfonso said I should be glad to not share the company of those dull soldiers and priests. They had no love for singing or poems, but they kept their wits sharp with games of chess. Alfonso taught me the tactics they used, the sly moves he learned from noble prisoners or Jewish envoys, or astrologers from Sicily and Algeria.

Alfonso liked to call himself "the Scourge of the Moors." My father was the greatest of the Moorish kings in the south, but he was far from the only one. Alfonso spent much time roving with his great army from one little kingdom to the other, exacting tributes and payments in exchange for peace. When an opportunity arose he overran the kingdom anyway and made it his own, in the name of Christ. Alfonso did not always win, I knew. My father had outwitted him twice on the field of battle in years past, but we did not discuss that. We did not discuss my own part in that ongoing war, where I too had been traded for a few months' peace, a pawn on their chessboard.

I told myself I was the only love that Alfonso and Mu´tamid held in common. My love for them both was God's way of placing something positive and good between these men so powerfully opposed to one another. I imagined my father and my husband loved me as I loved them.

I was a foolish girl.

The king returned that year and shuttled between San Facund and Leon for five months. Elvira was still suckling, but I the king took great interest in my body, changed as it was with having borne a child. I was a mare now, he said, no longer a filly. A hot-blooded Arab Barb, a proven producer. I did not much care for the likeness, but the thought apparently excited him, horseman that he was. My hips were wider, my breasts swollen. My nipples had turned from pink to brown, I bound my bosom tight between the baby's feedings, but my breasts went heavy with milk at the most embarrassing moments, as if they had a mind of their own. They tingled and burned and dripped whenever I heard a baby cry, any baby! Or if a hand simply brushed against them. It was mortifying to me at first, until Alfonso made a game of it, and touched and tongued at my great breasts to make me flushed and hot. The milk was sweet and wet, he pointed out, a gift from God. And so our bed smelled of love and curds, and the washing-women down at the river must have gossiped for weeks about the state of the linen. Nursing a child is known to make a woman infertile, but it was not so with me. Even as one baby suckled, another took root inside me.

The king left in the spring and rode eastward, toward Toledo. Hamid advised me then to write a document of wisdom to little Elvira, as queens in San Facund do not endure so well. (The prior himself told Hamid the king "shall surely ride his Arab filly into the ground.")

And so I wrote out all of the poems I could remember, and put them together with the treasures I had brought with me from Sevilla. Perhaps it was the spring, or the baby. It had been more than a year since I left Sevilla, and I longed for my mother. I heard almost nothing of events in the south. I had left without a backward glance, and even as Hamid and I traveled north with the Christians a great army of fierce Berbers was poised to cross the straits from Africa, perhaps to assist the Andalusian kingdoms against the Christians, perhaps to attack and overrun them. We felt lucky to escape in time.

King Alfonso had wrested his chests of treasure and a new wife from Sevilla, and seemed happy to turn his attention to other concerns while my father and his rich little kingdom fended for themselves.

I tried not to imagine what happened when the Berbers arrived at the gates of Sevilla... My father was a smooth-tongued negotiator. He'd dealt before with Ibn Tashifin, the Berber chief, and invited him to join forces with the Muslim Andalusians against the northern infidels. So far, the uneasy alliance had worked, but everyone knew how faithless each of the Andalusian kings was, how easily their treaties were forgotten when a better deal could be made. My father was as faithless as any of the rest.

Sevilla was the jewel among the little kingdoms, and the Berbers made no secret of their covetousness. When the tribesmen turned with hungry eyes toward Sevilla, Mu´tamid would meet them with a sword in his hand. He would never leave his city without a great battle. What then would happen to my mother, my sisters, my playmates, my teachers?

Little news came from the south, but reports of Alfonso's battles now and then mentioned my father and brothers. But for Muhammad they were still alive, still fighting alongside the brutish Berbers. The Muslims in the south were, for a season, united against the man whose bed I shared, whose babies I held close.

3
BELLS OF CASTILLA, POEMS OF SEVILLA

I am asked to write of my life in the courts of the great King Alfonso, but that is not possible.

I was never presented at the court of the king. I never traveled to Leon, where his grand palace stands and where all the great decisions were made. For three years I was kept in a few rooms of the royal apartments at the Monastery of San Facundo, and afterward in a house nearby.

Those years come back to me as hollow bells in the nighttime, and winter rain falling hard down the chimney, making the fire spit and smoke. Little Elvira chased balls and dolls and kittens over the floor for hours, laughing. She and the children of the pilgrims and the tiniest novices were the only ones allowed to laugh out loud in that solemn place, but joy bubbled up from between the bricks. My windows overlooked a cloister that opened onto many rooms. Sounds and voices carry well against all that masonry. I heard plenty of laughter, giggles, guffaws. I heard crying, too. Even sounds of passion.

Laughter, though, is like cabbage. It rises up easily, it is available almost for free. It is full of health, it lasts the year 'round. It sprouts up everywhere, especially when it's unwelcome. And some people find it indigestible.

Early on, the old prior Simeon was in charge of the day-to-day workings at San Facundo. He rarely spoke to me, but saw fit one afternoon in the garden to address my faults. He spoke in clear syllables, loudly, as if I were deaf: "Good lady," he called me, using his most formal Arabic, "it would please me greatly if you would assay to silence your jocularity whilst outdoors. It is not seemly here, so near the enclosure of the holy monks. We are unused to the sound of feminine laughter, and find it much distracting."

I was surprised to hear him speaking in the southern tongue. His accent and formality made me want to giggle, but I recovered quickly. I spoke to him the same way, enunciating each word, as if to a child.

"Your grace, I regret to inform you that laughter here is inescapable. I hear the holy sisters laugh over on their side of the wall. The workmen in the street outside laugh and shout and swear, in plain hearing of the holy men. And I hesitate to say so, but it is true: your holy monks themselves are often given to laughter. I assume they are filled with the joy of the Lord."

"Indeed," Prior Simeon said. "Perhaps my many years have dulled my ears." He was affronted, I could see. He nodded his head and left me. He was not accustomed to contradiction.

The following day I sent the prior a basket. Inside were three apples and a six-week-old tabby kitten called Isaac. Simeon returned the basket back to me empty. He ate the apples, but evidently did not eat little Isaac, who brought more laughter (and many dead mice) to the monastery's harsh round of fasts and prayers. I learned later that the prior, as he died, warmed his cold hands in the big cat's fur.

Poor Prior Simeon, I look back on how childish I was with him, and I regret that. He was a good man deep inside, suited to his job. While the abbot built their Benedictine empire wheedling from Alfonso all kinds of rights and taxes, the prior kept accounts of it all, using heavy books and unwieldy lines of C's, X's, V's and I's. He was an old man, but he rode out on his mule for hours every morning. He was counting, the serving ladies told me: The trees in the woodlots, the sheep in the fields. He paced-off the acreage tilled, calculating how much grain it would yield in July, how much flour it would grind down to, and ultimately, how he could take a greater portion of each process to his profit. Not his own. His monastery's. He was a prior, administrator of his particular flock of priests and monks and nuns. They had to be fed and clothed and educated.

I had no place in his little kingdom. I was an imposition, an embarrassment to him, but he would not argue with the king's will or the abbot's orders.

Priests, monks and nuns are God's chosen, set aside and elevated above the rest, often better fed and rested. Some of them work very hard, caring for the pilgrims and the sick, teaching and preaching in towns for miles around, overseeing farms and building projects. I heard of magnificent, saintly works, even miracles performed by particularly holy ones.

Some of the other monks, and all of the sisters, never step outside the monastery walls. They stay inside to pray and fast, study and copy out manuscripts. At San Facund, like here, they practice music on lutes and flutes, outdoors when the weather is fine. They teach one another to sing scriptures, then they practice across the cloister, throwing their sweet voices up and out against the walls. The songs bounce into the windows. San Facund was unusual, as in those days it was home to both nuns and monks, walled safely away from one another. Still, sometimes a sister sang a canto in her cloister, and a moment later a male voice, a monk, answered with the next line on his side of the wall.

For a Sevillana this was familiar play, we do the same with rhymes and riddles, improvising, playing, throwing quips between ourselves. The Christians do it musically, throwing holy songs back and forth across the choir and over cloister walls. As time went on I let their songs lift my heart upward, on the words of the ancient Jewish kings. And so we worshiped together inside our walls, but remained forever separated: Jews, Christians, Moors; monks, nuns, and princesses.

I think on poems, and so I shall write again of my life as a princess. I cannot describe the court of Castilla y Leon, but I knew well the court of the king of Sevilla.

My sisters and I were happy creatures, protected from all harm and fear, cosseted terribly by an army of nurses and maids. We lived in a dream. No children had more beautiful homes, or clothing, cleaner hands or fresher dainties to eat. As babies we were rocked in tiny hammocks under the shade of the lilacs and palms. As children we slept in marble rooms with the sound of songbirds and flowing, splashing fountains.

But before sleep, stories! My father's house was filled with music, poets, and storytellers. Great men gathered 'round our family's table each evening to simply hear the bedtime stories these artists spun for us children. Some of those songs became lullabies for my babies. I wish I could recall all the stories: genies, heroes, thieves and magic lamps, enchanted caves, hidden treasures! And all of them told in the most elegant verse... Verse, poetry, word-play. They were highly valued in Sevilla when Mu´tamid was king. His father was a poet, and his grandfather, too. Between them they made our home and our city a magnet for talented performers and writers.

My father played the lute and sang well. My mother was a great wit, a common woman who stepped into her queenly role with relish. She loved to make outrageous demands, and watch while my father's servants rushed about like ants to meet her whim. If things did not move quickly enough, she'd make fun of those who'd failed, in sharp, barbed poems. The steward who could not find figs for her in February would often hear himself skewered in the songs of the dinnertime entertainment... but she would soon enchant him again with a gift or words of praise.

My mother loved us. We were spoiled, dressed-up and taken out and played with. She taught the boys very early how to comport themselves with every class of people, as well as how to judge the quality of a horse or mule. We girls were shown how to spin flax and wool and silk into fine thread, and how to subtly scent our clothing, rooms, and bodies. I have her to thank for my sensitive nose, this woman who grew up in the mud along the river, the slave of a muleteer!

I think of my mother when I see ants trooping along the edges of the dining room. My sisters and I found a huge colony of ants living alongside the garden wall one springtime, and we spent hours in the sand around their nest, drawing roads and dams and little towns for them to navigate. My mother noticed us playing there, she hitched up her skirt and hunkered in the sand with us, and even introduced some water into the mix: suddenly we had mud to sculpt, and little lakes and ponds to build bridges over. That night, after we'd gone to bed, she had the servants sprinkle flour all 'round our works. In the morning we could see the roads the ants forged themselves, how they followed the contours of the miniature landscape we'd created and spread outward from their nest like the rays of the sun.

I once asked my mother to tell me about her life as a child. "I never was a child. Not until I met your father," she said. My mother, I'timad, is almost as famous as my father, but I do not know if her story has traveled so far as Leon and Castilla. So I will write it, too.

I'timad came from a village along the great river Guadalquivir. Her parents were slaves of a man named Rumaik, a mule-driver, and when she was born to them she too became a slave. I'timad was a brilliant little girl, and her parents went to great lengths to educate her, even though she had few prospects in life. Every day she accompanied one or other of her parents to their work, and thus she learned all labors that fall to women as well as how to care for animals, load up a cart, and charge a bit more for a delivery than it may be worth. This was why none of the vendors who came to our palace would dare hand over a short weight, or uneven change. My mother knew their tricks. She was not above entering the kitchen to count out eggs or weigh the grain and honey.

Still, I´timad forbade her daughters such vulgar pursuits. We were princesses, above such worldly details.

But back to my mother's tale: Best of all was how my humble grandparents taught I´timad poetry. In Al Andaluz in those days, everyone was mad for poetry, from the king right down to the street-sweeper. My father first went to rule in Portugal, when he was 23 years old—it's said you can stop a farmer plowing a field there, and he will compose a few stanzas of verse for you, on the topic of your choosing. And so the slaves of mule-drivers too gathered round their hearths in the evening to tell tales and throw out rhymes in a back-and-forth dialog fashion. One poet throws out a stanza, and his companion finishes the refrain with a fitting image—if he was any good!

The little girl became skilled at poetry, and at composing quick, witty, and colorful stanzas.

I´timad grew into a pretty young lady. Late one morning in June she and her friends took linen from the house of Rumaik down to the river to wash it—a big, heavy job that required lots of cooperation. So many lovely girls in the river meant plenty of men contrived to wander past, to survey the beauties of nature.

Among those strolling the riverbank were two handsome gentlemen dressed in beautiful clothes, laughing and teasing one another. They thought they were disguised as common merchants, but the girls knew who they were: the prince Mu´tamid and his best friend ibn Ammar! The girls smoothed their hair and stood up straight as the young men approached. Then they heard the men speaking—spinning poems!

A cool breeze blew, and the ripples on water inspired Mu´tamid to throw out a refrain:

"Behold, a breastplate welded by the breeze…"

And before the prince's friend could form a rhyme in reply, the mule-driver's slave girl, inspired the cold water she stood in, piped up:

"and fitted for a warrior, if it freeze."

Everyone stopped what they were doing. The princes looked at the slaves, and at one another, then burst into laughter. A slave girl, so quick, so poetic? How charming!

The prince called I´timad up from the water, asked her name, asked her who was her owner, asked how she got to be so witty. The girl in her wet clothes charmed him utterly with her replies.

Within two weeks Mu´tamid had bought her freedom, and her parents' as well. He set them up in a little house and spent evenings there, sharing poems and songs with the mule-drivers and washerwomen and his own soldiers. Soon his gifts and poems and tributes won the heart of the girl. They married, and the entire city celebrated the love-match of the prince and the witty washing-girl.

Mu´tamid had to leave home to fight battles with the other little kingdoms nearby, and sometimes much larger and powerful enemies. He was a fine leader and a fierce fighter. He did not lead his men from behind the lines, he was in the thick of every battle, a lion in armor. He stopped the fight when the time was right, and negotiated peace without needless destruction. For this he was respected by leaders in the other little kingdoms round about. Sevilla grew in power and glory. Mu´tamid became known as the poet king. And the poems he wrote to the queen were beautiful odes, romantic flights that still are famous in the south today. This one, written in Arabic, forms an acrostic:

*"**I**nvisible to my eyes, thou are ever present in my heart.*
***T**hy happiness I desire to be infinite, as are my sighs,*
*   my tears, and my sleepless nights!*
***I**mpatient of the bridle when other women seek to*
*   guide me, thou makes me submissive to they*
*   slighted wishes.*
***M**y desire each moment is to be by your side—speedily*
*   may it be fulfilled!*
***A**h, my heart's darling! Think of me, and forget me*
*   not, however long my absence!*
***D**earest of names! I have written it, I have now traced*
*   that delicious word: I´timad!"*

See how the first letter spells out I'tamid's name? What girl could resist him? Their palace was splendid, their company of the highest degree of wit and intellect. Their fame spread across the land.

In Sevilla the mosque was a long walk from the palace. My family did not spend much time there, even though my father spent a fortune transforming the old building into a showplace of blue-and-white tiles and stately trees. The teachings of Islam were central to our lives, but worship was something set apart for Fridays and Ramadan.

So life in a Christian convent, with its regimen of rituals and bells, was an adjustment for me. The abbey is the heart and soul of San Facund, and I lived in the royal apartments of the abbey complex.

Palaces and castles are plenty in the countryside of Leon, and they are scattered north and south through Castile— the very name of the place means "castle." Alfonso could have installed me in any of them, but he wanted me in San Facund. It was his favorite place, he said—he wanted to keep all his best treasures there, in that particular box. Alfonso was courtly. He was not a poet, and neither was he young. But he knew how to speak to a woman.

Compared to the lives lived by the people outside, the apartments at San Facund were beautiful, and much to my taste. I had a cupboard for my gowns and a chest for my linen, a fine wide bed with hangings to block the drafts and soft wool blankets dyed red. The mattress was not filled with rushes or straw, but with the soft down of geese.

Best of all was the garden. Thirty years before it was the monastery's main cloister, but the monks built a new one behind, and left the old one as part of the king's preserve. Ines, the first French queen (God keep her) brought fruit trees there from her home in Aquitaine. They grew in a circle 'round the well in the center of the courtyard. With the gardeners' care they bore abundantly: pears, apricots, figs, and apples. The apples were the finest in the region— Manzanas de la Reina, the apples of the queen! They are not the best I have eaten, but they were very good indeed, tart and firm and yellow. These were the apples I sent the prior. They are the apples I sent in gratitude to a lady in town who made a beautiful little cap for Elvira.

I still have that cap. It is woven with shiny thread, and when I tied the bow beneath Elvira's chin a pattern of smiling red lions marched over her head, from cheek to cheek. "Lions for the princess of Leon," the little card said, in Arabic. It is of very fine linen, woven tight. It suited the baby perfectly. She wore to Mass the following Sunday.

It did not take long to learn who made it. It came from Olaya, Hamid's Moorish widow. It was a wily political offering on one hand, and a sweet gesture on the other. I ordered from her straight away a beautiful wide linen cloth made in the same pattern, to fit the altar of the abbey church.

I called the pattern "Lion of Judah," so it was appropriately Biblical. A Jewish lion, woven by a Moorish woman, to honor the Christ. It is always so. Just look inside the reliquaries of the Christian saints: Whose cloth glimmers there, cushioning the martyrs' bones? It is cloth from Persia or Egypt, Tunis or the Atlas Mountains, the finest in the world.

The altar cloth was finished in time for the Easter Mass. Everyone knew the donor was me, because nothing was a secret in that town. The cloth was put there for the glory of God, but some did not see it so. There were small people there, angry, always hungry for offense. They did not approve of the king's choice of women, and they whispered my gift must somehow be a desecration. I found that offensive at the time, but now I know they were right, after all. Woven into the borders, in looping Arabic letters, were lines of Scripture. What did those beautiful letters spell? "There is no god but Allah. Muhammad is his prophet."

I was wicked in my way, but God blessed me. My little girl came so sweet and easy, and was healthy and happy from the start. Another babe was on its way, and the king had promised they would take their places as part of the royal family. But the children I made with Alfonso were not only heirs to Castilla. They were children of the Abadids as well. Their mother's memories and stories were just as worthy of remembrance and honor as their father's. I occupied my place with all the dignity I had been raised with.

Should God have mercy I will write more stories of my life in Al Andaluz. All these years later I still miss my old home. I do not suffer so much now, but in my days in San Facund I longed for my sisters and mother, and for the luxuries I left behind: almonds roasted in partridges and baked into pastries, orange blossoms, lemons and oranges for flavor, scent, color. Orderly gardens, full of fruit and flowers and fountains. Silk and soft leather, dyed to soft green, yellow, orange, red.

The cold stiffens my fingers, but I enjoy writing, it is something I do well enough. I never was a good needle-worker, nothing like my sisters, who could dress a family in silks in three days' time. Never was much good at weaving, or archery, or even poetry. But I was the eldest, the first born, the holy one who opened the womb of my mother. I carry her spirit more than the others—and she was witty and wise and curious, filled with the spirit of God. She made my vain, silly father into a noble man, a true king.

I believed I could do that, too, with the king God gave me.

4
SISTER ANA MEETS THE MOOR

Winter was sharply cold, and even though I was with child the prior did not believe in coddling me. I was given little oil and wax and firewood, so I wrote and sewed by the weak sun that pierced the slats of the window. The cold got into my bones, and my nose ran wet and red. The oldest and youngest died in the winter, dogs howled day and night, and the fleas bit fiercely. I stayed in my room, listening to what is said in the street and in the cloister below my windows.

Alfonso stayed away and sent no word. The roads flooded. In the evenings I was given wine to drink, good heavy wine from Burgundy. A woman in my condition was supposed to take wine, but I never became used to it.

In my father's house women did not drink wine. In lands where Moors rule, the vineyards left behind by the Romans and the old Christians were plowed under or left to wither. Only sensualists and wealthy men drank wine, and that was brought in from far-away vineyards. Christians are looked-down upon in Al-Andaluz, but they are tolerated. Upright Muslims avoid their villages and neighborhoods, full as they are of wine-shops, pigsties, smelly peasants and clanging church bells. My father, himself an experienced taker of wine, said the only good vintages Christians produce are drunk at the altar by their priests—And some say wine is why so many Christians flock to monasteries!

I learned in San Facund that wine on the altar is no longer "the fruit of the vine." It is transformed during the Mass into the blood of Jesus Christ. I did not understand what that meant, and I still do not understand it. My questions were met with suspicion and hostility—they still are! "It is a mystery," they say. Which means, "stupid woman, do not ask inconvenient questions."

If women are stupid, it is because no one bothers to school them. My mind is as agile as any man's, I read and write and keep accounts in methods unknown to even the best masculine minds for many leagues round me. Still, my grasp of history is not good. I know this great land, Hispania, was once a part of the vast Roman empire. They left behind their theaters, highways, and sewers. Then came Christian heretics from somewhere in the north, Visigoths, weaklings. My ancestors, the Moors, arrived from Africa some three centuries ago and easily overran the Visigoth Christians. They planted in Cordoba Al-Andaluz, a glorious kingdom of Islam. One Muslim king ruled the entire country, right up to the mountains in the north, but his kingdom did not last.

After several generations the overlords grew fat and weak. The Christians came down from the mountains and pushed them south again, and set up little Christian countries like Leon, Castilla, Galicia, Navarra and Aragon. Many Moorish families stayed behind in towns like San Facund. Some became Christians, for the sake of marriage or to escape the special taxes levied on "unbelievers." They were never truly accepted by the old Christians, the "pure-bloods," they still are not, no matter how saintly they might be. Moors live in their own neighborhoods, and keep to particular trades—these are Olaya's people. And so the land is scattered with Muslims and Christians, and sprinkled here and there with Jews as well.

We have lived alongside one another for hundreds of years, and the fighting has continued almost as long. Like the Christian kingdoms in the north, the land that once was Al Andaluz is full of religious strife and family squabbles. It is broken into several little kingdoms, each with its own beautiful cities, poets, doctors, armies, and spoiled royal families. Even now, armies from this taifa or that will sweep over their borders to burn towns, capture slaves, and steal whatever they can carry, with little regard to anyone's faith. Christian kings take their sons and armies and march south to wring tributes or wrest cities or province away from the dark-skinned infidel—or from their own brothers or cousins if opportunity arises.

War is not only a game for soldiers and kings. Daughters, too, have parts to play—we are gifts, peace-offerings, tokens of trade. Margaret, an aunt of my husband the king, was sent as wife to the Moor Walid of Toledo, to buy a few years of peace after the death of Al'Manzor. She was only a girl. I wonder if Walid give her a new name. I wonder if she gave him children, half-blood cousins of Alfonso. What became of Margaret? No one knows, or seems to care.

In Castile and Leon, generations of mothers have threatened unruly children with "the Moors out in the woods." Moors to them are apes, devils, wily and willful. It was difficult for the Christians of San Facund to trust me, a Moor—a princess and a baptized Christian notwithstanding—with their holy beliefs. It had not been so long since Al'manzor's men had passed through the district and burned the churches, houses, and standing crops. My grandfather's soldiers led their grandfathers away in chains to the slave markets in the south, never to be seen again.

Still, efforts were made to educate me in the ways of Christ. Soon after I arrived a nun was sent over from the adjoining convent to instruct me in Christian doctrine. Her name was Sister Ana, the novice mistress, and she was formidable. She stood straight and tall as a soldier, and her jowls and chin were prickly with black whiskers. She smelled of anxious sweat.

Her first words to me, that first day of instructions? "Sit down and fold your hands in your lap, and do not look into my face. Keep your gaze downward, to the floor."

I sat, but I did not look down. My face flared red with annoyance.

"Sister, with all my due respect, you forget I am not a nun," I told her. "If I wish to roll my gaze across the ceiling, I can learn my prayers just as well that way as I can from staring at your shoes."

She stood still and stared at me, her face scarlet. "You are not my equal, Doña. You shall speak to me with respect!" she spat.

"Of course I shall. And you shall do the same to me, Sister Ana," I told her. "Indeed we are not equals. I was

REBEKAH SCOTT

raised in a royal house. My father is a king. Mentioning inequities is below my position. I hope we can be civil, if not friendly. Because I shall not be spoken-to as a groom speaks to a horse."

She drew herself up into her black shell, and then folded herself onto the chair opposite mine. "Very well then," she said with a great exhale. "I suppose we should start at the beginning. Creation. The Genesis."

Every day for almost a year she came after Matins, except for when the king was in residence. She was educated and articulate, but completely lacking in imagination or curiosity. I must have been a penance for her. It took several days for her to understand that I understood her language perfectly well, even though I was from the south. I learned the northern Romance tongue from my cradle. Jimena, the nursemaid who raised me, was born in Burgos, she was taken away while still a child by Moorish raiders. I must have told Sister Ana that a dozen times.

I read the selections she asked me to. We discussed the saint or prophet or doctrine therein. Most of it was common sense: God made man, God made the heavens and the Earth, God appoints kings and princes and social orders, Man is made to serve God and not God for man. Nothing difficult. I was treated as a slow child, with small kindness and great condescension.

It was dull, but it was the only conversation I enjoyed in those days. I had no friends to visit, no lute to play. The days were long, and the lessons occupied my mind. I copied them out, to teach myself the Carolingian handwriting. I applied them to the monastic world around me. And so I asked questions, practical ones: Why the color

36

of the priests' vestments changed with the seasons; why the monks' heads are shaved on top; why the sisters must sing their Hours behind iron bars, like caged birds. I asked about the strange grinning creatures the sculptors were installing in the eaves of the new church, if they illustrated Christian stories.

Sister Ana had few answers. She said someone in authority would know, but she could never ask such questions herself. She preferred questions and answers in rote form, written out as litanies and repeated back. It seemed Sister Ana had never met a curious student before. Questions, to her, were impertinent challenges to her authority.

It is not so different in Al Andaluz. Hamid for a long time treated me with a similar condescension, saying I knew little of the world outside palace walls, that I was very spoiled.

Hamid was right. It was not such a good thing to grow up in a place where I could be curious, for in San Facund, and the greater world around me was populated by people who'd never asked a question in their lives, who simply accepted whatever was.

Sister Ana told me to take my questions to my confessor. He in turn told me he did not have time for "silly notions." Then the king himself told me not to exercise my mind over doctrines. The magic was done when I stepped into the water a Muslim, and stepped back out a Christian, he said. The rest was "just decoration."

I knew I was a Christian. I observed several sacraments: Baptism and marriage, confession and Eucharist, all duly done in the name of the Father, Son, and Holy Spirit. I was, as Scripture says, a new creation. I listened carefully to instruction and I applied it to my life. I tried to make sense of it. I wanted my children to be Christians, too, to better get along in this Christian world.

Aside from the garden in summer, the church was the best thing about San Facund. I loved the little Lady Chapel there, cool in the summer and warmed in the winter by dozens of candles. (I marveled at how royals wrote by the drafty window-light, to conserve candles, while the monks burned wax by the pound in empty chapels.) No one disturbed me when I was "at prayer," so I could stay in the chapel and let my mind wander until the cold crept out of the stones and up my ankles.

Christianity gave me an escape. When the weather was fine I joined in saints' day commemorations, or visited local shrines. I simply gave the order and a mule was saddled or a cart prepared, and Sister Ana and a guard were sent to ride alongside me. Ana wore her sour face, but she sometimes let drop a particular saint's day was coming up, that there was a local devotion... She enjoyed a day's outing, and she was a good rider. The people liked it, too. In the spring and summer of my first year in San Facund I went several times to such celebrations, and was cheered in the streets along the way.

That was how I discovered the Virgin of the Bridge, an ancient chapel along the pilgrims' road on the way into San Facund. We rode there on a fine sunny afternoon in April, on the eve of St. Mark—the festival started the following day, but heaven also credits those who arrive for the vigil. With us was a monk who grew up nearby, who greeted by name many of the people we passed. He showed us the bridge over a tiny creek (what passes for a river in those flat lands), and an encampment of ragged people along the banks.

The people there caught crabs and cut watercress to sell in town, and plied simple trades. Brother Esteban, a holy hermit, lived in a damp stone shack alongside the shrine, keeping the urchins from stealing whatever scanty holiness lived inside. We were welcomed, feted even, with river crabs roasted on a charcoal fire, and rough red wine pressed from the vineyard outside. The people were kind. They even offered us snails to eat! Two of them played beautiful music on a sort of flute, and the children danced.

The hermit was kind, revered by the poor of that place. He wore a grey habit like a monk, but his accent was odd and his eyes brown, like a Moor's. He told me God's love embraces all, from the highest to the lowest—and he asked me to pray for him! Imagine that! I laughed when he said that, but he only smiled. (His teeth were terrible, like a wolf's mouth.) "It's not a jest," he said. "I am expected to pray for everyone. Who but a princess has time to pray for me?"

We heard Mass, and rode home in time for Compline. The prior was furious when he heard. He came to my room and shouted at me, banging his fist on the table, warning me to never go to that place without my husband, that the river people were likely Basques, dangerous, idle criminals. "What would the king do to us if you came to harm?" he shouted at me. The monk who said Mass for us was beaten. I cried myself to sleep over that, as he only did what I asked.

I went back again later, though, when the monks again relaxed their vigilance. And every morning I prayed for the hermit Esteban, and the Basques. I still do.

And I pray for Don Bernardo, the abbot of San Facund, named also by Alfonso the exalted Archbishop of Toledo—the highest post in this part of Christendom. The abbot is a brilliant man. He grew up in the great monastery of Cluny, the Burgundian mother-house of San Facund, alongside a monk who became His Holiness Gregorio, the pope of Rome. Don Bernardo was connected to "powers unimaginable," Alfonso said. I was to pray for him every day, and treat him with utmost respect if we should meet.

Which means something, when said by the most powerful king in Iberia. Alfonso was enthralled by Don Bernardo. He stayed up late to write long letters to him, even as I slept in the bed beside him. He had their language and buildings, hymns and rituals brought to Castilla Leon and installed anew here. The cloth for his cloaks and the wine and grapes for his table were brought from there, and the very Latin words we say in church were imported from the great Cluny mother-house.

Men from Burgundy consider themselves the apex of civilization, even though they have no poems, no knowledge of stars or plumb-lines, even though their bodies smell of smoke and piss. They have little use for people from outside—everyone else is a foreigner, infidel, or heretic.

It was among these proud men my husband left me while he rode across the continent, wringing gold from the cities of the south, setting up churches in what once were mosques, securing the pilgrim path from east to west.

He was clearing the way for the Kingdom of God, and assuring his own eternal salvation. Every time he came home he brought more treasure, and more monks. Often as not, I met him with a new babe in my arms.

5
WAGES OF SIN

The second pregnancy was not so easy.

Summer started wet, and I was nauseated for weeks. I lost my appetite, and my body seemed shrink my belly grew larger. I did not leave the house, which was only proper. The woman who delivered Elvira had died in the winter, and as no move was made within the household to secure a doctor for me, Hamid engaged Yasmin, a fat Moorish midwife, a friend of Olaya's. She prescribed good company, fruit and laughter. Olaya then, with the abbot's permission, came weekly to teach me needlework and to pray with me the Christian prayers, to make me smile a bit. She was raised a Christian, her parents were converts, and she was crazy about Hamid! (In those days, among the classes of cattle dealers, innkeepers and farmers, no one much cared if a match was made among their faiths. Only the Jews kept to themselves.)

The king was due to stop in San Facund on his way to Leon. The midwife warned me not to share his bed.

The fields were full of poppies when the king returned, very late one evening at midsummer. He rode in on a huge horse, a gift from a Burgos mercenary currying favor. (Alfonso had not forgiven him, but he accepted the gift.) Up on its back King looked very much a hero, even though both man and beast were covered in the same mud.

Dozens of men rode with him, some of them ill and injured. And with them was treasure: Tributes, taxes from the south and the east, as well as Hamid's long-awaited tree-trunks and paving slabs.

The king wanted only sleep, and he wanted me. In the courtyard he barked out my name, even before he dismounted the horse: Isabel! I saw him down there in the torchlight, an island in a sea of moving horses and men and armor, all of them mud-colored. His men helped him down, removed his heavy mail and his greasy gloves. The kitchen boys kept a great vat of water filled above the central fire, another of Hamid's innovations, meant to keep me content. (My outrageous demands for hot water were the talk of the town, Olaya told me.)

I ordered water brought up. The king stripped off his clothes and sat on a stool while I bathed him with soft cloths, warm water, and soap scented with rosemary. It was our custom, a bit of Arab indulgence he found agreeable. The warmth relaxed him, the water took away a few layers of the dirt and sweat built up over months of travel and fighting. It was a way for me to see how his body had changed, to see any new scars or marks where his armor chafed or a knife had passed too near. This time, when I lathered his hair, I saw a bit of one of his ears was missing—he said a

Saracen witch had bitten it off in a fit of passion! Giggling, I knelt to wash his feet, ankles, knees.

He undid my hair and ran his fingers through it, held its length to his nose to smell its scent. As the cloth moved higher up his body, his penis stood erect. He grasped the shaft between his fingers and pulled it proud. With his other hand he touched a finger to the tip, scooped a dot of liquid onto his fingertip, and spread the seed across my lower lip.

Husbands are not supposed to be interested in women already with child, but Alfonso was not an ordinary man. Women are not supposed to kiss men there, but I knew what he liked, and what I wanted to do. I took him in my mouth and gently, with my tongue as the cloth, continued the same bathing motion on his root that I had used on the rest of his body. He shuddered, and a soft sound rose up from his chest. My mouth filled up with him, and he flowed over my tongue and teeth, lips and chin and throat. His penis went soft, his face paled and his head tipped back, his eyes closed. I was afraid. And beneath my rounded belly I could feel I was very aroused.

"Have I hurt you?" I whispered. "Is that wrong? Are you angry?"

"Dear God in heaven, Isabel," he said. "Maybe it is true what they say about Moorish women. You are... magnificent."

Perhaps then is when the damage was done, a sin committed.

We spent a single night together. For the sake of the babe Alfonso did not mount, as men do to wives in bed. We did other things, though—we used our mouths and hands

43

instead. The king had his pleasure, and he made sure I had mine as well. Perhaps these are whorish actions, performed only for carnal pleasure, outside the natural function of man and woman. I am told a woman already pregnant will have no natural inclination for carnal knowledge. But obedience is part of a woman's duty to her husband. I did not refuse Alfonso anything he asked of me. No wrong was done.

In the morning, before he left, the king knelt beside our bed and made me cry out one last time with pleasure. He slapped my flank as he stood up, and smiled at my high round belly.

"We're making sons together, Isabel," he said. "You Moors will conquer Leon in our beds, if not in battle." He kissed me, and was gone.

Six days passed. The pains woke me in the night, and labor came on in a terrible, painful way, nothing like the first time. It was too early, I was not prepared.

I rang for my ladies, I shouted out for someone to send for Yasmin. My hands shook as I tried to light a lamp, then I was overwhelmed with an urge to void my bladder. I raised my gown and bent over the chamber-pot. Something burst inside me.

A tiny form slithered out at once, I caught it in my two hands and held it close to my chest. My knees juddered, I knelt, the pot between my legs... the urge to push continued, harder. Something stung sharply—it made me want to howl. I put a hand down there, and felt another baby! Its head was poised... I took a great breath in, and pushed down with a great groan. It broke free and slowly emerged, turning as it came. It slid into the vessel, knocking it sideways.

I eased its little body onto the edge of the blanket, off the cold tiles. Its foot kicked. I rolled it over and saw a perfectly formed infant, a girl, her fists in balls and her black hair flattened wet against her long skull. Her eyes opened and looked blindly up at mine. Her mouth opened as if to speak, but she made no sound. I wiped at her, tried to lift her to me, but could not manage it with one hand. I shifted my position, tried to clear my legs from the tangle of bedding and clothing, my other hand still clutched against my chest, my body still streaming and straining, pushing out gray cords and liquid.

My other hand, I thought—the first baby! In the firelight I could barely see. I tucked the sheet over the lively one, then opened my arm to see the first, silent child.

It was not a child at all. It was more like a fish, a slip of pink flesh with huge round unopened eyes, scrawny arms and legs, tiny fingers, and the beginning of a penis. A boy. The start of a boy. It did not move. I cried out horribly. My hands shook like a crone's as I put it into the chamber pot, then lifted the bloody cords and envelopes of afterbirth onto it. The live baby I wrapped in the tails of my shift and held tight against me. She wailed. We panted and sobbed together. The women pounded on the door, but I could not move to open it, my legs and arms were shaking so.

I whispered to the Blessed Mother to help us. My pulse pounded in my ears. I seemed to fall asleep there on the floor.

I awoke in my bed some hours later, judging from the sunshine peeping in. My bloody clothes were changed, the blankets were tucked in around me. The air was heavy with smoke, sweet smelling incense that burned my throat. Martin, the new prior, and several other monks stood near. They picked up my ink pot and quills, they shuffled through my papers and opened my little box of flower petals and my perfume pots, sniffed at them. "Moorish," one of them muttered. Something heavy lay on my chest. A little bronze crucifix. I freed my hands from beneath the blankets, picked it up.

"Prior," I said. "Father prior. My baby," I croaked. My throat was so dry.

No one answered me. The men turned. One of them took the image from my hand with a sharp intake of breath. I saw the cuticles of my fingernails were dark with dried blood.

"Sir, what are your people doing here?" I said. "Why are those men looking in my things?"

"Quiet, Doña Isabel!" the prior snapped. "You must know what's happened. You have a daughter, alive but too small. And there was another creature produced. A dead thing. We have performed the rites to purify you, this room, this place. You are unwell. You must prepare yourself for death."

"My baby," I said. "Where is she then, the live one?" The men looked at one another. "It was taken to the sisters," a weasel-faced monk said. "They know how to care for infants. Women are forever leaving their bastards here for us to raise."

I felt myself color with anger, but I hadn't energy enough to give it rein. "That baby is the king's daughter," I told him quietly. "Speak of her with respect."

The monk smirked.

"And the other baby. Where is he now?"

"It will be burned. It was not a baby. It is the fruit of evil congress. Your sins, the sins of the king—that creature was the outcome of your coupling. The king will be informed. You must make your confession, Doña Isabel, prepare yourself. You do not want to die with this on your soul."

The anger left me. There were too many of them. The king was far away, headed south to fight again in Granada. I turned my face to the wall. My hands shook. The room was cold. I wondered if I might be dying, if perhaps they'd cursed me while I slept, or poisoned me. I could not let myself drift away. I opened my eyes and turned again to the prior.

"Bring me my little girl," I said, a bit too loud. "I must see her baptized, if she is so small and frail. She will be named Sancha, after the king's sister."

I cried then, and the men filtered from the room. Finally Yasmin brought watered wine and a bit of the vegetable broth that ushers in a woman's milk. She rubbed ointment on my belly. "Eat no meat for ten days," she whispered to me, "and nothing scented with almonds."

The door burst open and I woke again. Sister Ana was there, holding a yowling bundle in her hands as if it were a snake that would bite her. A priest brought water, said the words to ensure the safety of that angry little soul. Sancha was a tiny figurine, her fists tight and her face red and hungry. Finally they laid her in my arms. I spoke to her, and she knew my voice. She curled quietly against my breast and fell asleep there. The priests were sure she would die soon, and maybe I would too, if they were lucky. So they left us.

I told the Blessed Mother I would trade my life for Sancha's. I would gladly die if that would make her live and thrive. I was ready to leave this place, I told her. Maybe she should take us both.

But we did not die.

I do not know how many days passed, but Olaya and Yasmin appeared and disappeared along with my ladies. The sisters brought Elvira and Sancha each morning after Matins—Elvira believed her little sister was a doll for her to play with. The young nuns who looked after them were said to enjoy their work. I was happy to have a new baby to nurse. Yasmin said nothing is better for a newborn than its mother's own milk, and I always had an abundance. (It was then that Elvira stopped nursing.)

For many days I let myself rest. I did not cry any more. I felt numb, my mind full of slow pondering. The lost baby worried me, but I could not bring myself to call him "a fruit of evil congress." I did not confess. I did not receive the Eucharist. And so I felt my soul drying up inside me. If I died I would burn, but I did not have the energy to care.

One autumn afternoon in the garden, sipping mint tea and eating apple slices, Olaya and Yasmin took me in hand. Sister Ana was not with us that day, and I suppose they seized the opportunity.

"Listen to what we tell you. We are wise in these things," Olaya said. "Monks know nothing of women or birth or babies. You need to let the lost one go to his rest."

Yasmin nodded. "It is common for one twin to live and the other to wither," she said. "Your body is small, your hips narrow, there was not sufficient room for two babies to develop. Allah, may his name live forever, chose to take one. It is not for us to question."

She was right, I knew. My mother had miscarried at least one child.

"I have seen many of those little creatures not meant to be," gentle Yasmin told me. "It was in this very house that Constanza, the queen before you, may God keep her, lost two of her little ones. She lost five altogether, you know, after Urraca was born. The monks must know these things happen."

"And it is not for any of them to call you sinful for something that is normal. Something that is part of all women's lives!" Olaya said hotly. "They worship a virgin mother. They obviously know nothing of births and babies."

"Shh!" both me and Yasmin said—the noise of the fountain could not mask our words if we spoke too loudly. "I don't so much worry over my sins. I have little opportunity for sinning here in the monastery!" The ladies giggled.

"It is my bloodline," I told them, my voice low. They leaned in to hear better. "The monks probably didn't condemn Queen Constanza for her lost babies, but Queen Constanza was one of them. A Frank, an "old Christian," a near relation to Abbot Hugh of Cluny himself. But I am different, you know. The prior says my baby was monstrous because Moorish blood should not mix with the king's pure seed. That our union is unnatural and accursed."

Olaya sat up straight and spat on the pavement, incensed. But she quickly changed her mind, and her face creased into a huge grin. "The prior only just arrived from Burgundy," she said. "I suppose he's been walled-up inside a monastery for too long. It's just a matter of time before he learns that three-fourths of the monks in San Facund, and nine-tenths of the townsmen, are half-breeds of some kind or another. The town is full of Basques and Germans, Englishmen, Jews, Africans, Lombards, Gascons… We all are unnatural and accursed!"

"And monstrous, too, some of us," Yasmin quipped.

The ladies burst into laughter. Our joy bounced off the cloister walls and mixed with the fountain's applause. Someone above slammed closed their window-shutter.

"Make your confession, then. Tell them what they want to hear," Yasmin said, wiping her eyes. "Bring yourself back to life again, Zaida. Your little girls need their mother."

It was good advice, and a great comfort to me.

I finally spoke to the confessor. The priest absolved me, and my soul felt more alive. But my confession, once the prior heard it repeated, clearly was not acceptable. When I confessed thereafter the priest posed prying questions I felt were lurid and improper. He wanted me to say things that were not true. I did not cooperate.

The penances given for the little sins I did confess were much more strict than they'd been before. Responses to my questions and requests were curt, or ignored altogether. My food was neither fresh nor abundant, even though I was nursing a baby.

The monks had made up their minds about me. I know now that if I were not the king's consort, I would have been turned out of the town, as a wanton or even a witch. I am sure they told the king about the poor dead baby. God only knows what lies he heard.

6

I LEARN TO FEAR

The sun shone. Olaya came each Thursday, and we embroidered altar-cloths and napkins. She was handsome, a friendly, kindly lady with three children of her own to chat about. She was not the kind of friend one would expect of a princess, but I was not much of a princess in those days, by my own estimation. And I was lonely.

I recovered from the birth, and eventually the monks grew tired of questioning my bedroom habits. The king was gone all through the Autumn, up to the house of Este in France, traveling with Abbot Bernardo and many brothers of San Facund to their mother house in Cluny.

It is good for women to talk to other women. We spoke of children, birth, headaches, gardens, and weather. Olaya was a child of San Facund, she had never traveled farther than the cattle-sale at Saldaña, two leagues north toward the mountains. She was common but obviously well-off, the bright daughter of a convert cloth merchant whose only son was slow-witted. And so the girl became a wily trader, with her brother alongside. She was married young to a wealthy cattle dealer, and gave him three sons in quick succession. She learned his trade and tricks, but like so many vital men her husband died suddenly—an axle snapped and a cart overturned, and crushed him beneath its cargo. (Olaya wept when she told that tale, she obviously loved the man.)

Olaya wove and embroidered beautifully, and knew everything about cattle, sheep, horses, mules, goats, and swine. She could quote the going price of wool, stone, trees, cheeses, knives, hides, and linen. I had lived my life among these things and never once considered them as commodities to be bought and sold, each produced by a specialist craftsman, with a value relative to the others. She opened my eyes.

We did not often discuss matters of the heart, because we were rarely alone together. When Olaya visited, Sister Ana almost always arrived within moments, her sewing in hand, making the sign of the cross as she entered the room. She did not join in our conversations much. She usually sat quietly as a stone saint in its niche, listening. Sometimes her eyes traveled upward into the beams of the ceiling. I think she was watching for devils.

I kept my babies with me in those days, and Ana never was comfortable with them. Olaya brought them little toys, and made sure Elvira stayed well clear of the grate. They played while we worked and chatted.

Olaya was curious to hear tales of Sevilla and Al Andaluz, and for her I described the orangeries and almond trees, the gardens and river, how proportioned the buildings were, the tiled walls and pavements as rhythmic as a well-turned poem. I told about date palms, nuts, the tiny cheeses made just from cream and wrapped up in leaves, and how we rolled stems of rosemary and blossoms of oranges in our fingers to scent the air in winter-sour rooms. I recited poems now and then, but they were in Arabic. I think she and Ana found them over-long.

But they liked the tiles, the idea of corridors glistening white or blue or gold, with fountains in the center and channels of water running alongside.

"Wasn't it awfully cold?" Sister Ana asked. "What happened in Winter? And in the refectory, when men dine— the droppings on the floor. Isn't it slippery? What did you do for rushes? Do they use straw? Or blossoms, or leaves of the fragrant trees?"

I did not laugh at her questions like my sisters would have done. I smiled, and explained about the great number of servants, the abundance of water and brooms and mops, and pet cats that snatched up the scraps before they hit the floor. We dined in small rooms in winter, gathered round tables covered in heavy cloth, our feet tucked together underneath around great copper pans full of glowing coals. The weather there was nothing near as cold as it was in Leon, I told them. We did not suffer so much with it.

"But you are right about the slippery tiles," I said. "When it rains out in the courtyards, and the visitors track in the mud on their shoes and boots, well… everyone must step carefully, and stand very upright." I warmed to the memory. "It is difficult especially for horses and mules, and when the gardeners dig out a section of earth their poor beasts stagger and slip terribly on the walkways."

They listened, rapt. I thought of a story. "The day came a few years ago, when the tiles worked a wonder. A great Christian soldier from Burgos, the warrior El Sayyid, violated all custom and dared to ride his big charger straight into the throne room of the king of Valencia!" I paused, for dramatic effect. The ladies drew in their breath, waiting.

"The horse's great shoes slid on the shiny tiles, and the animal fell to its knees in the doorway of the of the king's formal chamber. El Sayyid was thrown forward, almost unseated! His bold gesture—a Christian, riding a horse within the city! Into the palace itself! His vainglory became his humiliation. His very horse bowed before the king!"

The pair of them looked at me blankly. A heavy silence fell over us.

"You will recall the great horse that King Alfonso rode into our yard this summer," Sister Ana said, with a bit of steel in her voice. "I am willing to wager it was a gift to King Alfonso from the same man, the same soldier from Burgos, Rodrigo Diaz. He is a great warrior, utterly devoted to our king. I have never heard of him ever losing a battle against the Moor. And certainly never of any such… humiliation."

Olaya looked nervous. "I believe Diaz is, these days, set aside. Estranged from the king. Something about raiding border towns without the king's agreement?"

"Rodrigo Diez is my mother's cousin," the nun said drily. "His wife Jimena is the niece of our King Alfonso." Olaya looked at me and widened her eyes.

I did not know what I'd said wrong, but I rushed to recover from my stumbling.

"You think this Diaz is the same El Sayyid?" I asked. "I have heard our king speak of "the Cid," but I have never heard him called Rodrigo. I know the man was at my father's court not long before I left. He gave my father some very bad advice."

There, I had put my foot in it once again!

We sat in chilly silence for a few moments. My mind raced. "If he is the same man, he is handsome," I said. "Heavy, well-fed. He is lucky, but not young. But for a Christian to be called "El Sayyid" in Al Andaluz, he had to be blessed of God. "Sayyid" means "Lord." He had obviously won great respect from the Moors."

Olaya cleared her throat. She picked up Elvira and kissed her nose. "Here among the Christian Moors the name is "El Cid." He pays his soldiers well, but expects them to take extraordinary risks."

"He is from Castilla. Those people are a law unto themselves," the nun said, throwing out an olive branch. "Now, you were telling us about the rushes. Do they have rushes on the floors in Sevilla?" she asked brightly.

The atmosphere lightened with the change of subject.

"They do that in the countryside, I think," I told them. "I traveled little. On my way to Almeria I recall some dwellings with straw or rushes on the floors... there is not much water in parts of Al-Andaluz, and for many miles there are no rushes. I found it strange when I came north, and found that straw and dried rushes were inches deep on the floors of even the royal chambers. At first I wondered if the servants were lazy, or if there were no brooms here!" I tried to laugh. "I had the ladies sweep out all my rooms, right away, and wash everything down!"

"It cushions the feet against the cold stones," Olaya said. "Common folk here do not have carpets or hangings."

"And rushes smell so good when they are fresh," Sister Ana added. "They soak up the drippings and droppings of the cooks and dogs. They keep the floor from becoming slippery. Not that anyone would ride his horse into the house!"

Not that anyone could, with the doorways and corridors so dark and low, I thought to myself. (I did not say that aloud.)

"Please, my ladies," I said, "this is not a judgment on the customs of this place…But after a month or two, especially in a room where food is made or eaten, or if wine is spilled, the rushes begin to rot. It seems to me their purpose is defeated, they become more of a menace than a benefit. By February they stink. And thank God for the sweeping of the house in Holy Week, because by then the dogs and the rushes alike are hopping with fleas!"

At that both women laughed. How strange I was to them!

They were strange to me. Many times I tried to pull Sister Ana into our chatter. I asked her to describe the baking of altar breads in the convent, and what her home was like, up in the mountains above Leon, and how the sisters' voices are trained to sing so high and fine. But when our eyes were on her she shrank into her black beetle-shell, and answered with short words—she couldn't imagine we'd be interested, she said. She was like a whipped dog, afraid of even a kind hand.

The monks trusted her. She rode along with us one fine morning to visit a new pilgrim hospital in San Nicolas, a village just east along the pilgrim trail. She rode well, and took charge of the visit like a person accustomed to giving commands. After inspecting the site and stones, she concluded the place was just right—near a spring, with good strong trees overhead for shade and wind-breaking, fertile bottom-land for a vegetable garden, and a fine sheepfold and flock to keep the place funded. Before leaving we stopped for prayers at a chapel just across the river at Villaverde, where a beautiful Blessed Virgin statue sat serenely on her throne, with a wizened little wooden man on her lap.

The country there is rough and wild, but full of lovely things. We passed by the Virgin of the Bridge settlement on our way home, and the people shouted and waved as we rode by. I waved and smiled, but Sister Ana pretended the people were not there.

She must have given a long, detailed report to the prior.

We spent many hours together, but Sister Ana did not care for me. I could not get to know her, because she would not let me. To her I will forever be an infidel. Now that she is in my mind again these days I pray for her. She is by now a powerful abbess, if she lives. I wonder if she ever prayed for me.

Prayers were her native tongue. Those afternoons when the light began to fail we put away our sewing and prayed a rosary together. It was then Sister Ana found her voice. She clattered over the prayers like a horse over a bridge. That rosary meant her time with us was almost over, that she would soon be safe again in her hard little cell, away from the noisy babies and the dark foreign women.

...

What is a foreigner? I was a foreigner in San Facund, but I did not like being treated as one. Even so, I treated the black-robed French monks from Cluny as outsiders. They were the interlopers in my world, even though it was Alfonso's father who first gave them the old monastery and town at San Facund, years before I was born.

Perhaps it was my upbringing, a princess raised to marry into another royal house. I held tight to my identity as a Sevillana, but when I promised myself to Alfonso, I promised myself as well to Leon and Castilla—to being a part of that harsh, wide northern plain and mountain range, and those hard, funny, crude people.

(This is a large, wide strip of beautiful rag paper. It is late, but the ink is good and summer burns long in the sky and my sisters are all out mowing hay, so I shall continue writing. I have thought long of these things. I will not be wasteful with the time and light that remains.)

Technically I was brought to San Facund as a prisoner of war, but I went willingly, with a smile on my face. King Alfonso saved me from a fate much worse than I suffered, and from the very first the king was kind to me. I did my best to capture his heart and his attention, and he enjoyed the novelty of a cultivated, sensual girl who met his jests with laughter and and his affection with equal ardor. Alfonso was not a brute. He was a noble, strong man, and a fine king.

How I came to love him I will maybe tell you later. But now I will tell you how I learned to fear him.

I was still quite young, very soon after our wedding rites in Salamanca. We were traveling north to San Facund, through the mountains. Alfonso and I still were learning about one another. I traveled from my home in Sevilla in the back of a horrible wagon, swaying and jolting, hidden inside hangings of smelly wool under a damp, grey sky. I grew sick of the stuffy wagon.

I knew how to ride, and my eye fell on a sweet chestnut mare, an Arab, that belonged to one of Alfonso's men. (It had first belonged to one of my father's soldiers).

When the king next joined me in the wagon I told him I wanted to ride, that I wanted that horse for my own. It was not his to give me, he said. When I began to pout and whine (how unseemly that is I am ashamed to write it!) the king struck me, not hard, and snapped at me to stop behaving like a child. My nose bled. The shock of seeing my blood made me burst into tears. No one ever had struck me, I wailed at him. How dare he treat me so, I'd have him whipped!

At that he laughed out loud! He pulled me into his arms and dabbed at my nose with his sleeve, and apologized for his pique—no one had ever shouted back at him that way, either, he said—never a woman! He said he would never strike me again, and he never did. I was careful to never give him cause.

I did not get the horse. I was instead given one of the mules sent with me from my father's palace, the one I had ridden the first day out of town, to the hermitage of San Isidoro, where I was made a Christian. If I was to ride, the king's steward said, I should cover myself head to toe in garments so the sun would not make my skin any darker, and so the soldiers and guards in the train could not look upon me.

These Christians, I thought, were more restrictive even than Berbers! But I had little choice. I did as I was told, and was able to ride when the weather was fine.

Only one of the women who traveled with us was familiar to me. I had hoped to bring with me Jimena, the nursemaid who raised me, a Christian woman of Burgos. I loved her, and hoped to restore her to her family. But she fled Sevilla before I fled myself, and losing her was a great blow. (She had babies of her own by then, her man a sailor from Cadiz. I pray she found safety and happiness.)

I was left with Aisha, a slave, a skilled cook and a baker of beautiful cakes and pastries. She was to improve the kitchens of my new home. She befriended a group of young nuns who traveled with our train. Their superiors had sent them north ahead of the wave of Berber infidels, men they knew were bent on burning convents and carrying off girls like themselves to fates unthinkable.

Their fears were well-founded. Many travelers made the journey with us, enjoying the safety afforded by hundreds of soldiers. Many slaves accompanied us, people born free in the south or the north, torn from their families when their villages were burned and pillaged by Castilians or Arabs or who-knows-who. (Jimena my nursemaid was captured twice and traded three times before she came to my mother's possession. Her ugly face, abundant bosom and facility with languages won her security in the palace nursery.)

Women did not travel at the front of the train, but far back amongst the baggage and tributes, well guarded. The nuns kept close to my wagon, where the guard was heaviest. They were pictures of propriety when we set out, intoning their prayers off-key as they plodded along behind. They spent just as many hours bemoaning their sore feet and aching knees. They should have had a priest or an older sister with them. By the time we met them, their holiness was wearing thin.

One wet day in the mountains I let the smallest of them ride with me in the wagon, the one who seemed to be suffering most from the mud and long miles. I regretted it instantly.

She was a practically a child, a lowborn girl of about 13 years from the desert near Badajoz. Her gray habit was spotted with grease and dirt, and her eyebrows, black and thick, met over her nose. She chattered about martyrdom and horrible Africans, ignorant of how her own features wore the stamp of the desert. She showed me a primitive good-luck charm she wore beneath her shift, a fist of twisted hair and bone. She wheedled and whined to see inside my trunks and baskets, but I told her No. She smelled sharply of sweat and dirt. I opened the flaps of the wagon, but the biting flies descended. And then, dear God, she took off her shoes.

I wrapped myself in an indigo sheet, right up to my eyes, to ward off whatever contagion made her stink so, and pretended to doze as she rattled on about praying the rosary three times through, three days in a row, how its magic power makes one's fondest wishes come true.

I did not invite her to ride with me again. In the following days the prayers and psalms from the nuns decayed to whining and complaints of my arrogance and hardheartedness—to ride along on a mule like a bishop while the Lord's handmaids walked in the dust behind my empty wagon! As if I would let that filthy rabble ride, seated on the very bolster where the king slept! I grew heartily sick of them all.

Like me, Aisha was re-named when we were baptized, but I do not recall her Christian name. She had no kitchen to occupy her, and so was ordered to help me with my clothes and washing throughout the trip. She did not like it. She only washed the linen, and brushed and coifed my hair, and tied me into my gowns in the morning, and this with the roughest of hands. Once I was dressed and installed again in my wagon or on my mule, Aisha skipped away to join the holy sisters.

One afternoon near Zamora we stopped to rest beneath a grove of trees. I awoke from my nap and needed water, but Aisha was gone. The little nuns just sniffed and giggled and said that Aisha was "indisposed." I called out for her, and in a few minutes she came striding up from the dry creek-bed, smiling and smoothing her coif. Tied fetchingly round her waist was a blue suede belt embroidered with acanthus leaves. It belonged to me. "Why are you bellowing, princess?" she called across the grove. I felt my face flush red.

"I am looking for my lazy servant," I said. "I want you to bring the water now. And I want you to remove that belt and put it back where you found it. Do not touch my things," I said.

On the path behind her a man appeared, up from the riverbed, unshaven and grinning. Aisha untied the belt on her waist and tossed it carelessly into the back of the wagon.

She took a step backward, shocked, perhaps, at her own impertinence. I slapped her face, knocked her sideways. The holy sisters gathered closer, making hissing sounds like a flock of geese.

"Bitch!" one of them whispered. They bundled Aisha back to the blanket where they had spread out their luncheon. She sniffled. Her soldier made a sign against the evil eye, then slipped away back to his post.

"Water!" I said, louder this time. "Bring me water, now!" And behind me, by the wagon, the groom brought round a bucketful. I turned away from the nuns and pushed up my sleeves and plunged my hands into the cold bucket. I splashed the coolness onto my face.

"Can't wash it away, darky," one of the nuns said, snickering. "Stained from birth. Mark of Cain," another ventured. "African ape."

I sent for the steward.

The king came to me that evening and saw I had been crying. I told him what had happened, what they had said. He did not laugh at me, or put down my sufferings to the wranglings of women. He did not make light of any of it. He did not stay with me through the night.

In the gray, drippy morning Aisha and the nuns were gone. I had to pin up my own hair and I did a poor job of it. We broke camp, but my wagon did not go far before the driver stopped again near a great cork-oak tree. I peeked outside. The entire train was stopping, circling round the tree, where the king's steward sat tall on his horse. He shouted out a decree: "This is what becomes of those who defy the king's authority and insult and rob their betters," he said.

Four soldiers shoved Aisha and her soldier into the clearing.

One of the men grabbed the front of Aisha's gown and pulled. It tore away easily, and she shrieked as her little breasts were exposed. A woman darted from one side of the crowd and snatched the coif from Aisha's head. Another woman knocked Aisha to the ground, while her children swarmed in to strip off her shoes and skirts. She kicked at them, screamed, until a soldier's well-aimed boot to her throat stopped the noise suddenly. The women seemed to know their part in this drama, as if they'd seen similar things before. I was transfixed. The crowd surged in, I could see no more of my servant.

The soldiers turned to their companion, the swarthy, sneering man, and stripped away his clothing as well. It all took too long. The pair of them, with cloths stuffed into their mouths, were stood up against the tree and bound there with their arms embracing one another, with the tree trunk between them. A roar of laughter broke loose when the terrified soldier soiled himself. A muleteer stepped up then and lashed each soundly with his whip, cracking it handily, showing off his skill. Blood and skin flew and splattered the people nearest the tree. The crowd sighed and roared as if everyone was inhaling and exhaling together, an odd singing sound. I turned away. I leaned out the side of the wagon just in time. I vomited in a most unseemly way.

We rolled on. Aisha and her soldier were left tied there. The sight of her is seared into my mind: Her eyes glassy and stunned beneath her undone hair, a scarlet cloth streaming from her mouth like a huge tongue. Her back was a mass of meat and fabric. Her ribs shone through like shiny white stripes, veiled in buzzing flies.

The night before, I learned, the nuns had been given over to the justice of the Church. One of the San Facund Benedictines, a priest, travels always with Alfonso the king, and he heard their case. The sisters were stripped of their habits and examined—strange marks were found on their flesh, evidence of their familiarity with evil. They were beaten and sent to the back of the train, where the whores service the common soldiers.

I have seen much blood and violence in my life, and even then I was not a stranger to cruel punishment. One garden at our palace had a line of pikes down the center, left from the days my grandfather displayed the heads of his enemies there. The walls outside Sevilla often were decked with the body parts wrongdoers. Many men and women, too, made their way through life with fingers, hands, tongues, or feet severed by knife or sword. Our household servants' backs were often striped in black and blue.

But never were any of them an outcome of my orders. Not until that day on the road. And so I pray for Aisha and her soldier, that their blood will not forever stain my hands. I pray for the simple nuns who I condemned, with my selfish anger, to lifetimes of sin. May our Lady hear my prayers and intercede for my soul.

And for the hard soul of Alfonso, who looked on that morning's horror as a simple dose of discipline for an army on the move.

Alfonso the king did not come to me much in the days after that, as I was unwell. When he appeared again I was much more humble and quiet. Alfonso said I should give my mule back to Hamid's care, that my husband now was now the proper animal for me to ride astride—I did not laugh. The wagon then was not so unbearable. The landscape was not so interesting. I took to the new mount, though, and with the king's careful schooling I learned to enjoy his particular equitation.

And within a week or two we arrived in San Facund.

7
Hamid is Praised

Hamid, who was known by the Christians in San Facund as Jacob the Moor, was very busy in the years I lived there.

I wrote before of the great projects he undertook in the city, draining the boggy streets and widening roads, bringing good water to every part of the town. He opened a forgotten Roman pipe and persuaded the waste of the town to flow through it and into the River Cea, downstream from the fishing weirs and the new bridge.

His greatest stroke, in my hearing, was combining the water-channel project with the monastery's bread ovens. The moving water created a steady draft of air between sluice and the fire-boxes, feeding the fires on air from below. Occasional flooding, done with gates and sluices, cleared away the accumulated ashes. It was a brilliant design, and people in town for the market stopped on their way in and out to watch it work.

Even the great Abbot Bernardo took note of Hamid's handiwork. It was not easy getting Bernardo's attention.

He was of Burgundian nobility, groomed at the monastery at Cluny, and had traveled years before to San Facund to be its abbot—Sister Ana attended his installation, back when she was a novice. When King Alfonso conquered the great city of Toledo he named Bernardo the Metropolitan Archbishop, in charge of all the churches in the realm.

The job called the abbot away from San Facund, and made him spectacularly powerful. Bernardo had princes from England and Lombardy crowding his chambers and clamoring for his favor, and he traveled much between his See and the Vatican and the Archabbey in Cluny. Still, San Facund held a special place in Bernardo's heart, and he came to stay when Alfonso's court settled for a season. He took a keen interest in developments there, and the prior kept him up-to-date with frequent letters.

The town was busy that winter and spring, as the court had come from Leon. The king was expected to arrive soon, and Abbot Bernardo came as well. One fine, crisp morning the abbot, the local nobles, and dozens of hangers-on muffled themselves in velvet and went out to tour the new works with the prior and Hamid. I stayed inside, out of sight, and watched as the servants laid tables of bread, cheese, and wine in the cloister for when the crowd returned. The fountain was drained for the season, so the clever monks filled its basin with apples. It all was just beneath my window, so I could eavesdrop!

The assembly was splendid in the winter sunshine, and the abbot was obviously the center of it all. He wore the same black habit as the other monks, but it was made of a fabric that flickered and flowed as he walked. Inside the sleeves and hood I could see, even from my narrow embrasure, a shine of silk. Hamid, too, was resplendent in a coat of dark green, and new boots of black calfskin. When the nobles sat down below to discuss what they had seen, I rejoiced to hear them sing his praises.

"Jacob the Moor, did you learn that water-and-fire business from observation, from seeing the remains of Roman forges?" Bernardo asked. Hamid began to answer, but it was obvious the questions were purely rhetorical. "We must adapt this drainage plan for our other foundations. I should like to see drawings," he said. "I should like to see more of this flowing water, and that hot water system in the kitchen! A marvel! Come with me to Toledo, man—I want to see that in my own house!"

"Your grace, pardon the query, but one does wonder," the prior said—"We are an order of austerity, reformers of the ancient Rule of Benedict... Are such luxuries suitable in a monastic house?"

The abbot waved him away. He pitched his voice deeper and louder, and the crowd quieted, to better hear what the great man said. "The hot water, my brother, arrived here on orders from the king—a man not given to austerity! We shall not contradict our Lord Alfonso, if he chooses to lay pipes within our walls, and comfort our cold feet with a warm bath in the evening... have you tried that, prior? Our Lord himself was an advocate of foot-washing, and not only once a year, for ritual's sake." The monks let themselves smile at this.

"Our Lord sends us his blessings from all sides—sometimes through the hands of the king, sometimes through the wisdom preserved in the desert, the remains of Babylon and Egypt and Rome," he intoned. "Let us sing for joy to the Lord, and shout aloud to the rock of our salvation. For is not our Lord a comforter, as well as a consuming fire unto our enemies?" he sang out.

The assembly grinned at one another and drank deep from their glasses. An impromptu sermon, delivered by a noted churchman, was great entertainment for a winter's day. Even better if it upheld their own appetites for small luxuries. The sun warmed the cloister, as the wine warmed their spirits.

"Look how He delivered back into the Christian hands of King Alfonso our city of Toledo, the ancient episcopal see of our Visigoth forebears! Look how he delivers unto us the clever men, once property of our enemies, men of knowledge and skill—should we push them away from us, refuse the gifts they bring to us? Should we then deny our abbey the innovation of the bread ovens, and our town the gift of clear streets and flowing water? These are jewels, my friends—jewels of practical use, to great men and lowly alike. Should we push away the providence our Lord makes for his children?"

"No, good abbot!" cried one of the guards.

"And so I shall not stand in the way of the Lord's will," the abbot said. "We should honor those clever men who bring their skills to us, even if they appear diabolical at first. We soon will understand them, improve on them, make them our own."

And with that he commanded the cellarer send a suitable thank-you gift to the home of the Moor Jacob. My heart sang within me, to hear my friend so praised.

Hamid asked one of my ladies to take some of the apples from the courtyard up to my room. When he returned home at the end of the day he learned the abbey, in its wise generosity, had delivered to the Moor's house a fine ham.

In the days that followed the abbot and his monks spoke freely when Hamid was present; clever as he was, Hamid was still, in their eyes, just a tool, a block of wood. No threat. Hamid listened when they spoke among themselves, and that is how we found out how cynically they manipulated Alfonso's piety.

He learned of their plans to wring more money from the merchants and landowners of San Facund as well as other abbeys strung out across Hispania: new taxes and levies to benefit the great building program at the Cluny mother house. Overjoyed as Bernardo was to be archbishop of the ancient See of Toledo, Alfonso's conquest of the city was proving costly in unforeseen ways. When Toledo belonged to the corrupt old Moorish emir, Alfonso and his father had exacted thousands of gold florins in tribute from the city each year, and sent the money to the monks at Cluny. Now that the city was in Christian hands, the money instead went to rebuilding the city walls, refurbishing the bishop's palace, and rebuilding the cathedral. Far to the north, Cluny needed to find new ways to keep the cash flowing, and Archabbot Hugh was counting on his brilliant Bernardo to somehow strike another vein of gold.

That meant making quiet alliances with powerful people. Arranging marriages, bartering, claiming and re-populating abandoned regions. And controlling the king.

From a chamber adjoining the sacristy at the Church of San Mancio, Hamid one morning listened as the great abbot dictated letters. There were great rambles about the new bread oven, building similar ovens in other towns, and somehow turning them into an "unquenchable fount of revenues, if the king can be convinced to assign us the right."

In the same letter, the abbot mentioned me.

"His majesty must be made to understand the fundamental uncleanness of their union, the unsuitability of bastard children," the abbot said.

"But we have been over this before!" the scribe complained.

The abbot continued. "Touch upon the fundamental blackness of the Moorish womb. It darkens the very skin of their children, does it not? Are not their babies born with a covering of hair, like apes? It is even possible his passion for this woman is the fruit of sorcery, that the king is bewitched. He should put aside this Moorish whore immediately, for the good of his kingdom as well as his soul. Who can tell what form the Lord's vengeance might take?"

The scribe said something unintelligible. The abbot retorted, "We shall wait until a more opportune moment to tell him of the stillborn beast."

So the king's priest was to tell my husband I was a witch. To them I was not the wife of the king, but only a concubine, producer of beastly bastard children. It sounds almost funny now, all these years later. But the man was in perfect earnest.

Bernardo knew Alfonso had little interest in babies and bread ovens, and had plenty of guilt, death, and betrayal to atone-for. The king would sign the papers presented to him, and seal them in a fog of applause and praise. The smiling monks kept Alfonso's eyes clouded with incense and penance, while they built an empire of their own with the lands and tributes he paid them.

8
DOLLS OF MUD

For months and even years I waited for news of my family, any news from the south. I heard rumors and whispers, but never any real information. I prayed for them each by name, every day. I wondered which God heard my prayers: Does the Christian God hear prayers made for Muslims people who bows five times a day to Allah? And if my father prayed to Allah for me, will He, for Mu'tamid's sake, bless his apostate daughter?

I knew I would never see Sevilla again. It was never again seeing my mother and sisters and brothers that made me ache.

My parents were still in the palace when I left. Agents of Ibn Tashifin, the Almoravid chief, were there at the court, eying the hangings and lamps, planning the pillage to come. Servants had begun packing up a few belongings, sewing their valuables (and occasionally some of ours) into their shoes and the hems of their clothes. One or two of them slipped away every month or so.

There was no great goodbye for me. Our agreements were already made, and there was nothing more to say: I had been bargained-away. Our city was surrounded by armies, and I was given by my father to the savage Christian, to buy time.

When Alfonso's great army moved south that year, my father and the kings of the other Moorish cities of Al Andaluz gathered together. They were tired of paying tributes to the greedy infidel, who settled his army outside their gates and threatened to destroy them if even more treasure was not forthcoming. Sometimes they raised an army and fought him, and sometimes they won—but never for long. The kingdoms were weak and full of corruption and disloyalty. No one was trustworthy.

My father and his fellow kings were faced with a final choice: to become fiefs of the Christian king, or to call for help from Ibn Tashifin, the crude Berber warrior from Africa. The Berbers were savages, illiterate desert-dwellers. Desert sand-storms taught them to veil themselves like women. They were as one with their horses, their swords were curved. They terrified their enemies with their perfect ruthlessness. It was better to have them as allies than enemies, my father said, and their hordes were expected within weeks. They would push back the Christians along the frontiers, but eventually (everybody knew) they would refuse to go back home to their desert. They would pluck for themselves the little principalities of Al Andaluz like cherries from a tree.

This is how history moves in Al Andaluz, it is how my father's grandfather Abdul Qasi Muhammad ibn Ismaíl ibn Abad became ruler in Sevilla. He was a zealous Muslim from the African desert who swept north to cleanse away the fat, feminine ruler and return the country to Allah. But the ease and abundance of Al-Andaluz fattened and corrupted him, and his son, and his grandson my father. It would be no surprise to see the Abadids swept away by another generation of starving fanatics from the south... or from the west, or north. It will always be that way.

I was a realistic girl, for the most part. Occasionally I heard the guards or soldiers mentioning my father or brothers—they still were fighting, or making bargains, buying time. Real news from Al Andaluz I am sure was kept from me.

Memories kept me warm when the nights were cold. I sang for Olaya and my girls the songs and poems made up around the table when we all gathered to eat. I told them about dates, nuts, oranges, grapes, fish roasted on a spit over a fire of wood—how we'd burn our fingers, how it stung when we squeezed the lemons over the hot fish.

Pregnancy and nursing made me miss my mother keenly, and I seemed to be pregnant most of the time! I loved my babies passionately, and I knew my mother would love to hold them in her arms and spoil them.

My mother was an expert spoiler of babies. I was her firstborn. My brothers Rashid and Mustafa Muhammad came next, and after them a gaggle of little sisters and another two brothers, too... my mother was a healthy, fertile woman, an ideal mother. But she was, before all else, my father's wife. Mu´tamid was her king. She flattered him outrageously, and gave him every opportunity to spoil her with displays of his power. Like the affair of the snow. (This, too, has passed into legend in the south):

The king and queen spent winters together in Cordoba, the old imperial city of Al-Andaluz, one of Mu´tamid's conquests. One February morning they awoke to see snow falling, covering the outdoors in a perfect white blanket. My mother, raised in the balmy climate of Sevilla, had never seen snow before. She started to cry.

"Oh, cruel one," she said to Mu´tamid. "How could you keep this pretty thing a secret from me? So many winters have I lived at your side, and never seen the snow! But now let me have snow every year, or surely you do not love me at all!"

Many husbands would laugh at such silliness, but my father was a king, and a poet as well. As an answer to my mother's wish, the Sierra de Cordoba was planted with almond trees. In the later days of winter the wind plucks their white blossoms and scatters them like a blizzard over the ground, leaving a snowy white frost on the fresh spring grass. And so there is "snow" each year in Cordoba, because of I'tamid!

Finally I will write the story of the "mud perfume," little Elvira's favorite:

My mother, once a queen, sometimes missed her lowly life among her friends on the riverbank and at the well. Soon after the birth of Rashid, my first brother, she and my father were taking the air in the garden on the riverbank. Father was overjoyed to have a son, and he showered I'timad with beautiful clothes and jewelry. But they were not what I'timad wanted. She stared out over the water at the women working on the opposite bank. They were working straw into the mud of the riverbank, using their feet to blend the ingredients that would later be formed into bricks.

"The mud is so beautifully squishy, it feels so slick and cool underfoot!" she recalled. "They are only making bricks, I know. But they can dirty themselves so freely, they can pick up handfuls and make little figures from it for their children. No one bridles at the mess or indignity, no one expects them to wear shoes, to keep their hems free from spots. How I wish I had some mud, too—but worthy mud, that would not make my king think less of me for squashing it under my feet."

So the king, who delighted in finding ingenious ways to please I´timad, called the steward of the house. The following day the second courtyard of the palace was covered in musk and camphor, ambergris and myrrh. When my mother was called out to see, the slave girls opened jars of rosewater and poured them over the costly essences, wetting them with even more fragrance. Mu´tamid himself knelt to remove the queen's shoes, and together they stepped into the scented mud. They squashed it underfoot, and made little figures out of it, and played like children there until night fell—the queen had her "worthy mud" for several days, and that patio carried the entrancing scent of it for years afterward. I remember it anytime the incense smoke rises in the church—it is the same frankincense and camphor smell I knew from my earliest childhood, when I played with the little

dolls my parents made that day
from that heady perfumed clay

in Sevilla, far away.

See? Even old nuns can write poems, if they are brought up properly.

9
I am Uprooted

This is a note I sent to Hamid. It was originally written in Arabic. I still have a draft copy, and so I translate it here. (Didn't I have beautiful handwriting?)

Esteemed Hamid:

Today I write in Arabic, to keep in practice, and because the monks take an interest in my writings these days. I told Sister Ana I am writing stories of my family, so my children will know of their heritage. She said that is "a vain pursuit." Poor woman. If she had heritage worth writing about I am sure she would be more sympathetic. (Her father is a noble, but their "palace" is, by Ana's own telling, surrounded by pigpens.) She wants to know where my ink and writing goods are from, where I got them, who gave them to me.

Sister Berenguela, one of the little nuns who cares for Sancha, dislikes Sister Ana. She says the woman is cruel, that she tries to trip up the novices with complicated questions, and beats them if they give answers she does not like. She singles-out the girls who were foundlings, or who come from poor families, or whose skin is dark, or whose speech is accented. Ana is kind to them at first, but soon makes cruel jokes about them. She pinches them, and laughs when they cry out. If they are clumsy, or doze in choir, she has them stripped and beaten.

I am not to trust Sister Ana, Berenguela says—Ana reports my sayings to the abbot. She would like to be relieved of duties here and go to the splendid new convent at San Pedro de las Dueñas, a place funded by her father, where all the nuns who live in San Facund will eventually move. But long as I am here Ana must stay and keep an eye on me.

I do not know Berenguela, but I think she is right. Sister Ana does not like to touch my girls, and for that I am thankful. I cannot bear to think of her being cruel to them.

Sister Ana informed me today that I must gather my things from this place and move to another home. The place I am sent is owned by the king, we walked round to see it. The house is solid enough, small and clean. It was built for a nobleman of Cea many years ago, his arms are carved in the wall outside. But the house is fearfully old-fashioned—I am sure you know it. The windows are tiny, no air moves through it, no light can penetrate. The ground level was a cattle byre, now turned to "sitting rooms," sister says—but the feeding troughs are still in the walls! It stands much too near the street of the butchers, I cannot not abide the noise and smell. And no one has told me why I must go. Have you heard any rumors, Hamid?

I know these were temporary quarters, but I have lived in these room for three years now. Your work has made this a comfortable nest for us, and now I suspect the abbot covets the best rooms for himself. How I will miss the hot water!

Hamid, do you know when the king might return? Have you heard any news from his people? Since he left France I have heard nothing of him—it's been so long! What will he say when he arrives, and I am not in his apartments?

With the abbot in the house Prior Martin no longer speaks to me, he sends one of his spotty boys to tell me what I must do. They leave damp wood for my fire, and my maids are harassed and questioned about my belongings and my comportment. I continue to appear at the chapel, but I no longer make my confession there. I know the monks do not have my interests at

*heart. Since you heard the contents of the abbot's letter
I wonder, even, about their loyalty to our king.*

*I am happy I did not plant trees and vines here, as I
would have to tear them up and take them away with
me when I go. I will leave nothing behind here might
benefit these monks. I am almost sad you did such fine
work on the water supply.*

*I go now to inspect the new house, and order hangings
and linens and perhaps furnishings.*

*Hamid, my mind keeps returning to the little hermit-
age by the river, out where the pilgrims enter the town.
where the hermit lives among the people. I should like
to improve things there if I can. You have the gold
bracelets still that I gave you before we left Sevilla?
Please, soon as you can, take some of them to the Jews
and with the proceeds draw up a proper chapel to be
built there, and a decent home for the hermit, and
perhaps a place for the pilgrims to wash and rest? It
would be a lovely place to plant my trees and vines,
seeing as I am shuffling from one house to another here
in San Facund.*

*It can be our project. We probably should not say too
much. I believe the chapel is owned by a noble family,
it is outside the control of the Benedictines—they do
not consider those poor people worth their trouble, as
they have no money or land. I wonder what the king*

will think of this idea. I wish he were here to advise me. More than anything, I wish I could do this myself, and not have to burden you.

Please ask Olaya to visit me early this week, I need her help with packing some things... might I have her bring some items back with her, to store at your home?

The lozenges she made for Elvira's cough worked beautifully; I should like to learn to make them myself. Little Sancha thinks they are candy!

Zaida

10
My Dowry Discovered

I decided the little house would not be bad, once it was scrubbed clean. I had it whitewashed inside and out, to destroy the nests of insects living there. An enterprising neighbor had installed his hive of honeybees in the barn out back!

The king and his men were on their way home, everyone said so. I determined to have the place in good order before my husband arrived. No one knew exactly when to expect them, so I needed to move quickly.

I asked the monastery steward to bring me items stored after I arrived, so I could consolidate my belongings. I expected only a footstool and the little head-rest and bolster I'd brought along in the wagon with me when I came north. But along with those came two great boxes I did not know I had—they evidently were sent from my father's palace after I left, and had come along in the baggage wagons. (This had to be my mother's doing.)

And so I found myself with a full dowry, gifts I did not know I owned! It was a beautiful day! I summoned Olaya to help me unpack the boxes. We made an inventory, which I copy here:

Here are the things I took away when I left Sevilla:

In my wagon I had:

a headrest of carved wood with gold inlay,
footstool with striped upholstery
a bolster
Six coifs of plain linen
An embroidered suede belt
Three gowns of linen
Three gowns of wool
Six binding sheets
Four pairs of under-trousers
Four blouses of various colors and quality
Hairbrush, pins, ribbons
Two vials of perfume
Four cakes of rosemary soap
a pair of slippers
a pair of common shoes
a pair of riding boots
a cloak of brown wool
2 pairs gloves
3 folios of rag paper.
5 cakes of ink.
17 gold bracelets.
1 pair gold filigree earrings

*In the monastery store were brought, with "Zaida"
worked on the lids in brass tacks:*

*A trunk of oak boards, bound in iron and leather,
studded. Lined with plain-spun wool fabric. Contents:*

*Three scarlet pillow covers, embroidered.
Two Almeria rugs, one red silk and wool, one
yellow-orange silk
A string of little copper bells, as used to announce
visitors
A leather bridle with silver ornaments, steel bit,
reins with fabric decoration.
A leather saddle with tree of beechwood, to match
the bridle
Two saddle blankets, rolled.
One quilted bolster, much compressed, in a canvas
cover.
Three bound exercise books, copied poems of
Mu'tamid of Sevilla.
Two tiny daggers, copper with scabbards of cabo-
chon inlay. Decorative.
Five large cakes of dried figs
Five large cakes of dried dates
One water vase, clay, beautifully thrown, from
Majorca*

Inside the lid, sewn beneath the lining:

*Fourteen beautiful sheets of parchment, used once
then scraped down.*

*A vellum sheet with the Abadid genealogy drawn
in a fine hand.*

*A trunk of oak boards, bound in iron and leather,
rubbed with wax to repel water. Studded. Contents:*

*Two pillows
Six linen coifs, finely spun and embroidered
Six blocks of starch
two sets buttons: 6 pewter, 6 silver
A wooden casket filled with 45 goose quills, cut for
writing but untrimmed
Five skirts, silk over and linen under, in colors
Five woolen skirts
Six linen binding sheets
Six pairs linen under-trousers
Ten linen shirtwaists, two each in white, red, yel-
low, green, and brown
Six linen blouses, white, with ribbons
Two nightcaps, silk
Two sheets, raw silk backed with quilted linen
(water-damaged)
Two pairs slippers
Two pairs sandals
One pair riding boots
One heavy wool cloak, with hood.*

*Sewn into the linings of various items (by my moth-
er's hand!)*

*four earrings of jet and silver,
a necklace of glass beads*

ten gold bracelets
two vials of poppy seed syrup
17 silver coins with al-Mu'tamid seal pressed in.

I had a fortune in personal goods for years, and never knew it was mine! The boxes were stored in an alcove directly beneath my window, and I never knew they were there. The seals were broken, they obviously had been inspected, but only cursorily—the common bolsters and pillows were laid on top of the rest. I was amazed no one had spirited them away. I never would have missed them.

Thank God. These proved to be boxes of Divine Providence, treasures from an old existence that made possible my new life.

I gave one of the ribbony blouses and a vial of poppy syrup to Olaya, a copy of my father's poems to Hamid, and sent a pair of slippers and a silk nightcap to Yasmin. We carefully folded everything else again and returned it to the boxes. I sent them over to the new house with the rest of my things and tried to hide my delight.

That bonanza proved how beautifully the king had provided for me. I possessed a wardrobe of clothing and goods, and I had no need of any of it! Still, I admit to great delight in opening the boxes and pulling out and unfolding all the beautifully made things—once so common to me, suddenly exotic in cloth and cut and color. And the scent! When I opened the clothing box the scent of frankincense and camphor filled the apartment and lingered for hours. Delicious.

I entertained myself with thoughts of what I'd wear when the king arrived: The pretty blouses with the many-colored shirtwaists and the skirts dyed to match them, a different combination each day, with the soft slippers and their little spangles. Over time I had adopted the monastic spirit of San Facund, and dressed like a Castilian lady in grey and brown and black. I decided to remind my king he had married a Moorish princess. Olaya and I cut down one of the dark green skirts to make little dresses for Elvira, and I wore a matching dress to Mass the following Sunday.

It was a mistake.

II

The Unclean are Cast Out

Royalty in San Facund wear clothes of every hue and fabric. Lowly folk, unless they are traveling jugglers or whores, wear garments dyed the colors of the earth: brown, black, dun, dirt. And thus I learned I was regarded in San Facund as a rich foreigner, but not a royal person. The common took their cues from the priests, and it was ever more obvious what the priests thought of me.

In my ignorance and vanity I wore a jolly green dress and yellow under-blouse to Sunday liturgy, and dressed Elvira in a matching gown. (Sancha still was too small to go out.) It was the Feast of St. Felix, the church was chilly. I climbed the narrow steps to our bench in the king's gallery, and heard a stir of what I thought was admiration from the crowd below. But at the end, when I gathered Elvira in my arms to leave, the noisy crowd did not part to let us pass through the great doors.

I always had a guardsman nearby, but that morning he was lounging on the porch outside. He did not call for the people to move. My lady went ahead of me, but had to jostle aside the people. They chattered to one another, unusual behavior while still inside the church. They did not look at us. Something was wrong.

Finally we could not move further. My lady called out to the guard, who finally stood up and shouted for the folk to "Move aside, make way for Doña Isabel."

The people moved. They went very quiet.

When I stepped over the lintel a hand came from behind. It grabbed the right sleeve of my dress, and tore it seam-wise off my shoulder. A hot voice near my ear shouted "Slut!"

The crowd rounded then and came alive, spitting and shoving, women and men, familiar faces, people I thought I knew, people I thought were friendly to me.

"Dressed like a whore, and in the church!"

"No lady this! Take her round back, Jacques, let's have a go!"

"How do you dare, Arab?" The hand that tore my sleeve grabbed at my coif, then raked at my skin with sharp nails.

Elvira felt the bolt of fear pass through me, and wailed. I heard words, shouts. I dodged fists and hands, bending my body over Elvira's.

"Slut!"

"Get out, bitch. The whores don't dare come here."

"King's bitch, king's get!"

"The Moors, in our very churches, Moorish whores!"

Other babies cried, women shouted, fingernails poked and tore at my eyes and dress, hands grabbed at Elvira, at my sleeves and hair, and pulled at the cloth of Elvira's dress. A body behind me, a man's body, pressed against my back and shoved his hips obscenely against my bottom, his hand grabbed onto my right breast and squeezed, bruising me. An old woman spat horribly, spotting my skirt. I screamed. Someone tried to pry Elvira from my arms but I would not let her go.

Finally the guard shoved his way through to us, bellowing and throwing bodies aside. From the church behind us the priest appeared, his habit swirling round him, his eyes all alight with righteousness. I thought he'd come to save me. He raised his arms and shouted,

"How do you dare?" The hands let me go, the crowd unraveled out the porch and into the street. Elvira howled, but the shouting stopped. The priest was in a rage, his face was purple, his mouth was wet, spitting. "In the doorway of the church! The very doors of the sanctuary! Dear God, we shall have to re-consecrate the entire... any violence? Any blood spilled? Any blood?"

Everyone stood straight, considering, taking stock of his physical state. I realized I was sobbing.

"No blood, father," my guard told him. "I will take her safely back."

"Get her out of sight!" the priest spat. "Is there no one to teach this... this Moorish woman... how to appear as a Christian, in a Christian church?"

Voices snickered. The priest turned on the people. "And are you rabble any better than Moors, assaulting one another in the very doorway of the sanctuary?"

"Not one another. Just her. A Moor, a whore! The king's whore. And his child, the child of a whore!" a cheese-seller shouted, and many voices shouted alongside. "Look at how she is dressed. And the child the same! He asks too much, keeping this bitch here!"

My guard turned and back-handed the man with his mailed fist. He crashed to the ground. A woman screamed. "Think twice before you insult our lord the king," the guard said. He grabbed the hair of the man standing behind me, and slammed him skull-first against the great pillar at the door. The priest laid his hand on the guard's shoulder. "Shed no blood here," he told him. "I have enough work to do."

The priest turned to the crowd, ignoring the two men bleeding on the ground at his feet. He did not tell the crowd I was a princess, worthy of respect. He did not even deny or condemn their insults. He said only "this woman is among us at the king's command. She is the king's affair, and none of yours. Go home now."

I was in a fury, but I would not let anyone see that. I walked with as much dignity as my torn clothing and screaming baby would allow, back to my quarters. The guard and my lady trotted to keep up. The guard trotted with his sword drawn, and a troubled look on his face.

I ordered hot water, but it did little to wash away the sting. Poor Elvira was terrified, so I cuddled her to sleep before I let myself cry. I opened one of the trunks and pulled out some of the scented things, spread them out across my room, wrapped myself up in the useless, luxurious garments my mother had packed for me.

I let myself despair, just for a little while. I read the love poems my father had written to my mother. There was no such love for me. My king left me behind for months, in a place where my royalty meant nothing, where even the

94

priests and cheese-mongers saw me only as a black whore, the king's mare. I was deeply insulted.

But at least, finally, someone in San Facund was telling me what they really thought.

Sister Ana came to my room the following morning, supposedly to pray the rosary with me. She peered closely at me, perhaps to see if I was bruised or injured. She cast her eye on the pretty red carpet rolled out on the floor, alight with leaves and flowers in a complicated symmetry. She had never seen the like, she said—she got down on her knees and put her fingers into the nap. (It is still with me, it is here on my floor now—it is silk and wool, from Almeria.)

"It is beautiful. Why is this here?" she asked.

"It is mine. It came with me from my home, a gift from my mother," I said.

She stood up and brushed invisible dust from her hands and habit.

"It is wrong to keep it here, to be trodden underfoot. It is too fine," she said. "It is worthy of a lord, or a bishop."

"A king, maybe?" I snapped. "Or an abbot. Yes. Maybe there is something about me the abbot might find acceptable."

The nun did not understand sarcasm, or just brushed it away.

"You are right. Let's roll it up straightaway, and I will send a man over to collect it," she said. "The abbot will be delighted. He can put it in his quarters or maybe the sacristy. Or even behind the altar in the monastery church!"

She began to roll up the rug, her face alive with greed. "Beauty best serves the glory of God, not slaves of the flesh," she said. And when she rose, she smirked at me. I inhaled. I made my voice as cold as I ever have heard it.

"Woman, do not touch my things," I said, placing my foot on the rug. "Leave now. Do not come back until I ask for you."

Her face went red, but she went.

I was readying myself for the move anyway, and Sister Ana only made it easier to go. I re-packed the trunks, kept the rugs aside to use in my new little house, some sheets and blankets, some of the clothing. I wrote to Hamid, asked him to send a cart and some men to move my things there, to lay a fire, lend me a few servants. I had to get out of that monastery.

I had much to do to prepare for the king's arrival. Hamid, of course, took care of everything, he and Olaya and a few of the men from the riverbank. My timing was not good. Hamid and Olaya were hard at work on other projects, but within two days I was settled in my new home, dark and low but clean. Hamid took away the trunks. I was not to worry.

Digging had begun at "The Virgin of the Bridge," the hermitage. My bracelets had fetched a surprising sum, and Hamid coordinated the project with a waterworks he had underway in the Juderia—he was making a special bathing pool for them, and the Jews are as keen on bathing as our people are. Hamid and his crew were always digging or burying something, no one questioned him for a moment. He ordered stone, beams, pipes, and sent them to this place or that one.

He planned a simple set of buildings, stone below and in the arches, brick above—all the world of San Facund is

made of adobe mud, all but the monastery and the churches, where stone and bricks are brought in from near and
far. Our chapel would have a single apse and a lobed altar,
and space enough for 20 worshipers. The hermit would
live in a single room alongside, with a hearth and a chan-
nel of running water. A long enclosed porch would provide
a hearth for pilgrims. Water would be piped through the
walls, with stone sinks on each outlet and channels to carry
away the waste. The community outside would have a covered washing area, and stone pavement in the miry places.
That was the plan. I never saw the finished work, but some
have since told me it is a marvelous little place, a jewel on
the way to Santiago.

Hamid hired a few of the resident Basques to help. They
worked like horses, he said, chivvying the others along and
ensuring the lines were kept straight and true. They saw
the building as their own. The hermit did not like the plan
at first, but agreed to pray and fast on the matter for a day
and a night. Hamid told him the improvements were the
will of God as revealed to me, that the Hermitage of Our
Lady of the Bridge could be a great aid to pilgrims on the
Way to the great shrine of St. James, as well as "a beacon to
the dispossessed," (a term I am sure he learned from Olaya,
who loved such poetic flourishes.)

And so it was agreed. And so the hermit, I suspect, was
the one who sent to my house little parcels of figs and fresh
river-crabs.

Among the cowherds and vagabonds who lived by the
bridge was Brother Lucas, a sculptor of some talent. He
was a disreputable fellow, a runaway from a monastery
in the mountains of Leon. Hamid asked him to carve an

image of a Virgin of the Bridge to stand in the new chapel. The rascal named a ridiculous sum, equal to the price of three dressed stones. We told him we would pray about it.

Winter arrived with a coating of ice. I was left alone, almost ignored. The little ones stayed in the warmth of the nunnery during the night, and played with me in the day. My guards made no comment when we rode out on clear days to see the works along the river. I made sure to wear dark colors and ride inside my wagon. I no longer worshiped at the monastery, but at the parish church of the Holy Trinity. Like the ragged folk at the bridge I made my confession not to a black-robed, tattling Frenchman, but to the holy hermit.

It was good to have a project, something to draw my mind out of San Facund. It was worthy, and the cost was not high. No one, not even the abbot of Cluny himself, could question the goodness of what I did there... and no one seemed to give it much notice. I was sure Alfonso would be pleased, he being so devoted to church-building.

12
THE KING IS GENEROUS

The king and his men returned from Burgundy on a clear, cold morning. The wagons were piled with things from that country: wine and cheese, skins and ink, books and messages and treasures and treaties, and a swarm of new monks to further tangle us all in the Cluniac net. The people of the town ran out to meet the troops and wagoners. Wages were paid. Taverns filled up, even the monks sang their songs with extra spirit.

My little house was not fully furnished, but it was very white and clean. In the smaller of the two rooms upstairs I unrolled the two beautiful rugs, and they covered the wide floorboards from wall to wall. I laid two big bolsters down on them, and draped two sheets from the ceiling to make a little bower. All afternoon the ladies warmed water in the massive stone fireplace. I bathed the babies, and had a bath myself.

Alfonso had never seen little Sancha, so I dressed her in a gown cut from a scarlet wool coverlet. I mended and put on our green dresses that had so outraged the locals. I undid my usual braid and had my hair pinned up in the fashion of Sevilla, with its full weight falling down my back and shoulders. I rubbed twigs of lavender between my hands, and dropped them into the bowl of bathwater on the hearth. I waited for the king for many hours.

When he arrived he was not at all himself. He'd eaten too much, he said. He wanted no wine, but poured himself a cup anyway. He took Elvira on his knee and sang a little song, but she was tired and not cooperative. Sancha was asleep. Alfonso showed little interest in her. The nurse took them away to their beds at the novitiate. The maid poured more hot water into the basin, and left us alone.

Alfonso bolted the doors behind her. He made the sign of the cross, and turned to me. He looked terribly tired, and older. I did not embrace him as I always had. He sat down in the chair opposite mine, too far away to touch.

"Isabel, what is wrong with you?" he said. "You look as fine as I have ever seen you, but you do not seem...yourself. Have you been ill?"

I did not know what to say to that. I felt a cold wave of fear wash over me. The monks had told him God knows what, and for months.

"Is it the dress? People here do not like the color green, I think," My voice shook a little. "Here only whores and witches wear colored cloth. I didn't know. The prior must have told you how we were treated, how Elvira and I were attacked at the church. If I have shamed you, I am sorry."

I swallowed. I waited.

He sighed. "You look beautiful, Isabel. Perfectly beautiful. If I am ashamed, it's for what I have done. For bringing you here to live. You are too beautiful and strange for this town. They were right. I should have left you in Sevilla."

"If I had stayed in Sevilla I would likely be dead now," I said. "Or a slave. Do you not see the hand of God in any of this?" I asked him. "Elvira, and little Sancha?"

"No, Isabel. Listen. You remember, in Al Andaluz…the great pink birds that fly overhead in the spring, clouds of them, their necks long as a swan's?" I nodded, smiling at the memory.

"You are one of them. It's as if one of those strange pink birds came down to live in a yard of ducks and hens."

"And pigs. It is true, Alfonso. I am a stranger here. It is not always easy for me."

"I regret bringing you here," he said quietly, not looking at me. "These people have no idea what you are. You are too foreign. They will never see you as a noblewoman, even if I beat them with the flat of my sword. This is wrong. We are wrong, being married like this. You are suffering for my sins. We cannot continue."

I swallowed back the lump in my throat. "Remember, Alfonso. I chose to come here. I came willingly," I said.

"I should not have been so impulsive. My eyes and hands were full of blood the day I saw you. I had been drinking. I wanted you. You were a princess, and they were always telling me that only a royal bride would do. So I found myself a royal bride. One to my own taste."

"You are a king. You are not supposed to act for yourself. You must consult with dukes and and generals, no?"

"The archbishop, the abbot. They are experts in these things. Their men told me this was a mistake, a sin."

"A sin against nature," I interjected. "A violation. Abomination.

Alfonso continued, as if I hadn't interrupted. "You were not suitable. But I took you anyway. It made me happy to see how angry they were. And when I kept my promise to your father, and actually married you! Oh, theatrics, the tragedy!" He smiled at the memory of it.

"You think you did wrong, marrying me?"

"The wrong was not in marrying you. I would have wronged you, and your father, had I not married you. The wrong was bringing you to San Facund. You and your children, living among these people who find you so offensive. Most towns would not care, Isabel. Moors, Jews, whomever…we don't really care, so long as everyone keeps his place. You may have been fine in Leon or Burgos or Toledo, where all our people manage to live together. But the abbot, and San Facund? No. I put you here to defy him, to show him this is my town, in my kingdom, and I marry the woman I choose. Of course as soon as I leave he punishes you—your beauty, and the babies, too—the joyful noise we made, right there in his very house! Scandal! It is a slap in his face, every time he sees you, and your belly, and those babies! And so it is my fault you are punished. My fault you are harassed by louts—they take their lead from the monks."

He looked around my dark little room. "Look at this place. This is wrong, in so many ways."

We sat quietly for a few moments.

"Do you think they are right," I asked, "that a Moor cannot be a worthy wife for a Christian king?"

"Isabel, you would not believe the nonsense I've heard," he said, smiling ruefully, swallowing the last of his wine. "They think I am an idiot. The best yet is that you have bewitched me… You, little Isabel! It would be funny if it were not so impossible. If they were not God's servants I would break their necks."

"They told you about the dead babe. The one that arrived with Sancha?"

"The monster? The demon?" he sighed. "Isabel, I am sorry. I should not have touched you that night. That is a judgment on me. For my lust. For the incontinent lust I have for you, even when you are big with child."

"He was a baby," I said. "Stillborn. A boy. They do not want your sons to come from me."

Alfonso finally looked into my face. "Was it a son, Isabel?"

"Almost a son. It was very small," I said, holding out my cupped hand to show the size. "Not even really a baby yet. But certainly not a devil. A tiny, tiny boy."

If I kept on I would cry, so I picked up the basin and brought it to him. I opened the front of his shirt, and dipped a bit of fleece in the warm water. He stood, and let me open his clothes, and remove them. He let me do as I always had done. But this time I wept as I washed him, and I let my tears fall on his skin.

The king stayed with me in the little house for more than a month. The days grew longer. He had furnishings brought in, and a new bed for Elvira with cherub-faces carved into the corners. They frightened her so she could not sleep there! Finally we drew little mustaches and furry eyebrows on them, and all was well. The four of us stayed together like a common family. We prayed a rosary each evening before retiring, the entire household on its knees. We sent the girls to sleep with the nurse in her cozy room above the barn. She kept a warm fire going there, and we would not wake them with our noise.

My bedroom had a huge, heavy bedstead, but Alfonso and I stayed in the little bower on the floor, like Bedouins. We delighted one another, stretched out like cats for hours, coupling and folding together our hands and eyes, lips and limbs.

One afternoon Alfonso had me stand in the weak sunlight by the window while he examined my body. He had me describe the births of babies, how it feels to have a tiny person moving inside, and coming out as well. It embarrassed me, but he asked in great sincerity. I told him what Yasmin had said, that everyone has a difficult pregnancy now and then, that I still was young and healthy and could have many healthy babies in coming years, sons and daughters, should the king deign to give them to me. At that he laughed, and pulled me over onto his lap. He liked me best pregnant, he said. He loved me that way, round and pink. He wanted to fill me up with children.

He said it sadly, though. He said we should keep trying, we only needed to get it right one time. And meantime we could keep our blood and bodies warm, and make all the noise we wanted there in our own quiet house, doing what husbands and wives do together in their rooms. I felt his sadness, I felt already the end coming. But I also felt the desperate heat of Alfonso. He thought he was running out of time, that perhaps this was his last chance. He set about

me desperately, like a ram set to tup a single ewe. Well beyond what was required.

The season was mild. Hamid and Olaya came to feast
one afternoon, and we rode out to inspect the works at The
Virgin of the Bridge. I wore the green dress that day, too,
and no one in San Facund uttered a word of criticism. I was
beautiful, my cheeks rosy and body flush with good love.
Out at the bridge the people cheered, ran from the riverbank and work site to help us dismount. Elvira squished
in the mud with the other children, dirtying her clothes,
laughing and clapping her hands.

We did not see the holy hermit that day—he'd hidden himself away in some long penance. The carver Lucas
worked on corbels of strange birds with curved beaks. He
showed us the great trunk of wood that would become the
Virgin of the Bridge image, soon as his price was met.

The king seemed pleased. Hamid referred to the chapel
as "ours," and "we" did this or that, but I did not tell the
king how the work was paid-for. I learned that the people
of that little hermitage gathered each evening to pray in
the structure that soon would be a chapel. And when they
prayed, they prayed for us.

The king was seen inspecting the works, so of course
the monks of San Facund raised a fuss about the project.
The land had belonged to an old family, its ownership had
been disputed for generations. The king's tax collectors had
seized it, finally, and its fields went uncultivated, its buildings fell derelict. But a little community was springing up
there, and the monks at San Facund did not like any enterprise outside their control. Abbot Bernardo told Alfonso

he should cede that parcel, too, to the abbey, so the chapel would be properly administered.

That night, after some wine, Alfonso told me how the conversation went. I shall try to remember it properly:

"There is a holy man there now, a Brother Esteban, a monk of San Miguel de Escalada," Alfonso told the abbot. "I am surprised you do not know him, he is ministering to the poor, right outside your door. You know of our good brothers at San Miguel, don't you?" the king asked. "Most of them from Córdoba, nowadays. But for hundreds of years they've been in Leon, since the times of the Visigoth hermits. Their caves are still there. Holy men, very holy. Artists, some of them, and mystics."

"Of course I know them," the abbot muttered. "And their old rites, outlawed. You, king, should go there soon and enforce your ordinances. I understand they still do not speak Latin in the Mass, two decades after the proper Roman rite was taught to them!"

"Latin, Mozarab, rituals!" Alfonso said. "You churchmen! You want to own the church and all the people inside, and every word they speak! Let's leave this one. Talk to me of something else."

"But sire, the Virgin of the Bridge…"

"Leave it," Alfonso said. "Let the people there have a single, simple chapel to themselves. I have already paid to have an image carved for the altar. The charters are already being drawn up. Leave this one, Bernardo. I want to keep them sweet and happy, up at San Miguel."

This was the best gift Alfonso ever gave me. It still delights my heart to know that little church in the fields is its own establishment, with royal patronage.

Alfonso spent hours early in those days at the abbey and the law courts, and in the afternoons we sometimes rode to see the roads and sewer-lines and waterworks. We went to Mass one Saturday morning at the monastery, and afterward strolled out to see the beautiful and efficient bread-ovens at work. Abbot Bernardo was there, crowing over his latest prize to whomever would listen—though he turned his back when he saw me. Not only did he have the most up-to-date bakery in the country, but from that day forward the monastery held exclusive rights to bake bread in San Facund. Alfonso had signed the papers a few days before. And so the plan that Hamid heard hatching had succeeded.

It was not without precedent. The monastery years before had built weirs in the little river Cea, and by royal edict the residents were forbidden to fish there. Any fish eaten in the town had to be bought from the monks. On Fridays, when meat is forbidden, the poor lived on gruel or vegetables rather than pay the monks' prices—which somehow rose higher as Friday approached, and peaked in the Lenten fast. Olaya said a traveling peddler who sold salt cod in the market was pilloried for his crime, condemned from the pulpits of the churches, his cart seized by the righteous men of God.

And so the baker-monks were given the same royal privilege their fisher-brothers enjoyed. Every housewife and hostelry with bread to bake, even those with ovens of their own, could use only the monastery's ovens for the job—at a price, of course, in loaves, flour, or money. Anyone who dared to bake his bread elsewhere faced a steep fine, or even a beating. The abbot told us all this in a jolly mood, and thanked loudly St. Honoratus, patron of bakers, for inspiring the scheme. (Honoratus was from Amiens, he made clear. Another holy Frenchman.)

We took home some bread, but found it no better than the usual. People will someday rise up against these arrogant priests, I told the king. He laughed at me, told me life is much harder for peasants in other places—men who worked monastery land were exempt from military service, and could always borrow grain and flour from the monks if their crops failed or famine threatened. I should be more kind-hearted to those poor celibates, he said—the French know about governing, farming, and forming alliances. I should watch and learn from them, so someday I could rule a monastery of my own.

I need no lessons in evil-doing, I told him.

The king gathered his army again at the end of the month, and went to confer with the Duke of Lara. They joined forces and marched to Aragon, and on to the south to Zaragoza or Granada or Córdoba. I do not know what he sought there. With the court gone back to Leon, the abbot decided to return to Toledo, where he could finish the renovations at his palace.

I rode out three times that summer with Hamid and my guard to see the works at the bridge. The chapel took shape, the pavements were a wonderful improvement over mud and ruts. Elvira loved to visit there, where she could play with other children; tiny Sancha grew fat. Olaya's oldest boy was apprenticed to Lucas the carver, so we visited the workshop to see what griffon or mermaid was emerging from his collection of stumps, stones, and timbers.

Many women in San Facund were made pregnant that year. As expected, the king left me with child too—a fine healthy one, carried high under my ribs and kicking from the very start. He left me five fat coins, too, with his profile printed on one side. I wish he had stayed and enjoyed that summer of happiness. The monastery was a thousand steps from our door, but the monks left me and my girls in peace, busy as they were with their new schemes.

I was not complacent. I grew up in a court full of schemers. I knew those jackals were not finished with me. And I knew when the king had said goodbye this time, he meant perhaps forever.

That dancing baby was my last chance.

13
POET KING AND GRAND VIZIER

And so I should tell you how I ended up in San Facund, and why I was glad to go there.

Somewhere in these papers is a story about my happy days as a girl, in a white palace along a wide river, with sisters and brothers and a wonderful, wise mother. All that was true.

I did not write much of my father, though, except the stories of his poetry, his courage in battle, and his love for my mother. You will remember the story of his meeting of my mother, along the river where she washed linen with her friends.

With my father that day was Ibn Ammar, his best friend and the greatest poet of our age. Ibn Ammar, like my mother, was born of lowly people, and rose to Mu'tamid's notice because he was talented, witty, and very intelligent. He was a born politician, a lover of beauty and comfort, a jewel in a court of glittering talent.

I will try to keep this short, it is difficult to write, as the story does not always show me or my family in a good light. I give thanks that no one bothers with the writings of women (rare as they may be!) and that this document is to be hidden away.

When they were young men, Ibn Ammar and my father were lovers.

I know how unnatural and shameful this sin is viewed here in the north. In the south, in my youth, this was not unusual among the young men of the court. I understand the prince of England now is of that sort of man. Convents and monasteries are full of such pairings.

The king and Ibn Ammar met in Shilb, the paradise of Portugal, when my father still was a prince and Ibn Ammar a beautiful, upstart courtier. They inspired one another to beautiful poetic heights, they traveled together and drank and enjoyed the company of women, but everyone knew they were most devoted to one another. My grandfather did not approve. He sent Mu'tamid off to faraway provinces and battles to separate the two of them, but it only made their love deeper.

My father met my mother while in the company of his friend. Ibn Ammar was amused by her, he looked upon her (my mother said) as a man of taste looks upon a greyhound—as an elegant toy. He did not count on the love that grew up between my parents. Ibn Ammar remained close to my father, but as they matured their devotion shifted to battles and government. When my grandfather died and my father took the throne, Ibn Ammar was made his Grand Vizier. The kingdom grew, with Cordoba and Jaen and Murcia falling under Mu'tamid's sword.

Kings and courts are full of intrigue and treachery, it is the price we pay for our luxuries. The kingdom of Mu´tamid was large and rich and beautiful, but torn with petty feuds and religious wrangling. Sevilla was always a tempting target. To the north a great cloud gathered, a mighty Christian army whose ferocity equaled anything Mu´tamid could muster—led by a young lion called Alfonso!

And to the south, across the straits in north Africa, stood the rich Arab kingdom of the Almoravids—fierce, strict Muhammadans who view poets with disdain. My father and his allies sometimes paid the Almoravids to cross the straits with their Berber army and help fight their wars. But once they arrived, the Africans did not always go away again.

My father, and his kingdom, were caught between them.

My sisters and I knew little of these things. We were protected from the worst of the ugliness, but we could not avoid reality altogether. Our brother Rafiq, my parents' firstborn son, was killed when he was only 14 years old, victim not of the Christian wars, but of local treachery. My father's brother was taken in battle and ransomed at great cost. He was a merry man, full of jokes and repartee when I was small, but he returned to us broken, his spirit shattered, but worst of all grotesquely speechless: his tongue was cut out.

In Sevilla itself criminals, plotters and thieves were punished horribly in the public places, their heads or hands, tongues or fingers cut off, their families sold, their houses broken up and their goods carried away by strangers. My father's court was sparkling and humane in so many ways, but our very palace was the scene of awful death. In the beautiful old hammam in our garden my grandfather arranged to meet three rival kings—only to have them suffocated inside. (My father had it pulled down and rebuilt in a more modern style.) We lived in a fantasy of light and poetry, but reality in Al-Andaluz is as brutal and vicious as anywhere in the world.

My father inherited large tracts of countryside, and conquered many more. He needed good men to help him govern them, but the men appointed wanted only to seize the land and power for themselves. Letters and documents passed constantly from hand to hand, and palace plots were constantly coming to light. As time passed Mu'tamid spent more time on politics and fighting and less on poetry. His spirit grew tired, but he did not set aside the physical delights of youth. He filled the palace with musicians, with singing slaves, boys whose beautiful voices were matched by long shanks and slender bodies.

My lute instructor told me one of these boys, a slave with strange blue eyes, first damaged the long friendship of Mu'tamid and Ibn Ammar. My father's friend brought the boy one evening to a revel as a gift for the king. Much wine was drunk that night, and when the party ended Mu'tamid begged his friend not to leave. He asked him to stay with him in his room, as of old, to share with him the beautiful boy.

This they did. And in the deep of the night, after all were fast asleep, Ibn Ammar was three times wakened by a harsh voice crying in his ear, "Unhappy man, one day he shall kill you!"

Ibn Ammar was terrified. He slipped away from the pillows and hid himself under a mat in the garden, planning to wait until dawn and flee that very day to Africa and safety. (We Moors are a superstitious lot, we believe in dreams and prophecies.) Ibn Ammar fell asleep out there, and in the morning the king, missing his friend, had the palace searched. Ibn Ammar was found half-naked in the bushes. Shame-faced, he told his story.

The king said it was the wine that whispered in his friend's ear, not spirits from beyond. (Many, like my teacher, believed it was the beautiful boy who'd cried out, paid by a jealous courtier to break up the bond of the king and his vizier.) The matter ended in laughter, at least for a time. The royal friends once again took to disguising themselves as commoners and haunting the low places of the city, sampling every kind of sin, uncovering plots and hatching a few of their own.

In those days their poetry and repartee reached new heights. Ibn Ammar wrote this for Mu´tamid when they were young men, a token of his devotion:

> *Alas, my prince, I have no power to hold you,*
> > *Not so, not so*
> *But wheresoever you journey, I pray*
> *As you are lightning to my darkened way,*
> > *Grant me to go*
> *Ever with you; you cannot say me nay*
> > *For it is fitting so.*
>
> *Take thou a sailboat swifter than your wit,*
> > *And I will be*
> *The ripple running astern of it.*
> *Ride alone, with no one beside you anywhere!*

And I will be
The strong wind tugging at you by the hair, —
    You shall not go far from me.

But when at last your paradise is won,
    the last long mile
(forgotten in our time) you then shall run,
With sword in hand, to pay your journey's cost,
    Paid in a smile,
Reclaiming wasted days and moments lost, —
    I must then leave you for a while.

And while I remember these sweet poems, I also remember the bitterness of Ibn Ammar's wit. He was not a great believer in religion, and looked with disdain on men of faith. One Friday on the way to the mosque for prayers, the vizier and the king saw the muezzin climbing the tower to call the city to prayer with the words of the Adán (ah, writing this fills my own heart with homesick longing!) Mu'tamid the king was inspired to throw out a line of poetry for his friend to complete:

Hark, to the hour of prayer the muezzin cries, he said. He looked to Ibn Ammar to continue the refrain with a witty reply.

Trusting that God forgives his many lies, Ibn Ammar said, mocking. The king was not pleased. He came to the holy man's defense, saying

May he be blessed, since by him the truth is sung,

To which Ibn Ammar replied,

Blessed is he, provided he believes his tongue!

Perhaps it was his humble origin and his grand ambition, or perhaps his great love for my father was abraded by all the dalliances, the houris and singing boys. Perhaps having to share him with my mother was too much for Ibn Ammar's jealous spirit. He wheedled with my father to take other wives, to blunt I´timad's influence, but my father had love enough for only one woman.

Ibn Ammar wanted all Mu´tamid's love for himself. Thwarted in this, over time, I understand how Ibn Ammar grew bitter and cynical, even cruel—it is a bitter thing to have to share your lover with another! It showed itself in little ways, easily ignored or explained-away.

My little sister Qamar had poor eyesight, and Ibn Ammar, during a session of joking and fun, told my mother she should have her drowned, like one does with a damaged puppy! He once brought gifts for all of us children from some faraway town, leather thongs strung with pretty glass beads. He tied them snugly on our wrists and went off with my father somewhere. And in the next hour the bands drew the moisture from our skin and contracted, tightening down on our little wrists like manacles, biting into our flesh until our finger-tips turned blue and we screamed with pain. The nursemaid snipped them off with her seam-cutter knife. My mother was affronted. Soon Ibn Ammad and my father returned, and mother took me by the wrist and we marched out into the patio, tears running down our faces.

"How could you do such a cruel thing to innocent children?" she shouted at the vizier, holding my bruised wrist under their noses. "What kind of man would give a gift that would maim a child?"

"But dear girl, those bracelets are famous!" Ibn Ammar cooed. "They come from Cartagena, on the coast, they are made of a unique sort of leather—the Romans used them to bind prisoners to the pillory. I thought the children might find them amusing."

He looked more toward my father than to us, watching for his response. Father was drinking. He made a slow, slurred rhyme:

How strange it is, the gift you bring
would bruise the daughter of the king!

Ibn Ammar's eyes sparkled. He was on familiar ground. The king was giving him an opportunity to redeem himself. His response rolled back with lightning speed:

A leather thong, a wooden bead
unto a false conclusion lead!
The bracelet? Harmless! The giver reckless,

And my mother cut in, her voice hot —

if only it had been a necklace!

The men laughed out loud. "I'timad, no harm was done," my father said. "Ibn Ammar did not mean to hurt you, Zaida. He has no children of his own, and he knows nothing of toys. I am sure he is sorry," he said. "Aren't you?"

"I would not dream of harming you, dear girl," the poet said. He did not look at me, though. He stared over the edge of the parapet, as if he'd spotted something much more interesting on the river.

We were dismissed.

My father did not see clearly. We children were simply part of his legacy, his glittering possessions. Ibn Ammar, and my mother, were perhaps the only two people in his life he saw as truly human.

When I reached age 15, my father sent me east to marry the emir of Murcia. It was an alliance of himself with another powerful house, as is done in the courts of Al Andaluz—and in Castilla as well. I was to have an easy time of it there, as the emir was an old man, with four wives already and many concubines. Many of his children were older than me! No one asked me what I thought of it, and it did not occur to me to comment.

That is why, when Mu´tamid's Grand Vizier Ibn Ammar was sent as ambassador to visit Murcia, I traveled along in his train. It was a great adventure to me at first, dressing in silks, riding in a pretty cart hung with dyed curtains and the royal pennants, making eyes at the guards, and learning how to throw a proper tantrum. My poor nurse Jimena was beside herself—I'd always been well-behaved at home, but now, outside the oversight of my mother, I pushed my limits.

I meant no harm. I had no idea what kind of trouble I could have come to out there, as in those days I was innocent of the ways of men and women.

The vizier had six great strong guards assigned to keep me safe, eunuchs, men who feel no desire for women. They were slow-moving men, but jolly. I enjoyed teasing them, but I respected them, too.

In those days, when we stopped in a village to rest or change horses, it was common for the more daring of the local women to come offering water or fruit, to twitch open the curtains of my wagon to have a peek at the princess. I usually saw them coming, and sometimes I'd pull aside my veil and giving them a huge smile. One day I hooked my fingers on either side of my mouth and twisted my face into a horrible grimace, and the poor lady screamed and ran away! News must have traveled ahead of us, and the same evening a boy approached the wagon for a look at "the monster princess." Ali, the smallest of the eunuchs, broke his wrist for him. It was permissible for women to see me, but men? No. Not even boys.

We were only a week into the journey east when things went wrong. It was a steamy hot night, I needed to relieve myself, and I let myself out quietly and slipped to a clump of bushes nearby, only two or three steps. I had a bowl for that purpose inside the wagon, but sleeping with it nearby, in the stifling heat, was unthinkable to me—my nose then was terribly sensitive to bad smells. I did not want to wake Jimena and have her take away the basin. She was bad-tempered in those days, too old for traveling. She would not have let me go outside at all.

I was slipping back to the wagon when a picket guard, a soldier, appeared out of the dark and called a challenge.

"It is me, the princess Zaida," I whispered aloud. "Just using the bushes! Quiet, man!"

Two of the eunuchs suddenly appeared. Jimena's head popped from the wagon, and she began to cry. "Where have you gone, girl?" she wailed. "What have you done?"

"I am right here!" I spoke softly to her. I stepped up to the wagon and slapped her into silence. We went inside. I tried to settle back into sleep, but within moments the eunuchs came back.

And so, in my bedclothes I was taken to the smoky, noisy tent of the Grand Vizier Ibn Ammar himself. A raucous party was winding down, bowls and cups lay on the rugs and laughter filled the air. I did not fear Ibn Ammar. I had grown up with him in the house. He was my father's friend and my protector on this journey. I'd been strictly instructed to treat him with proper courtesy. So when I entered I made the customary greeting to him, as a princess acknowledges a ranking courtier. I touched the fingers of my right hand to my opposite shoulder, bowed halfway, and opened my right arm in a graceful sweep, then stood straight and tall.

Several of the people inside made full bows in return, but several more did not move at all. Ibn Ammar did not rise, nor kneel as is the custom—he was sprawled on a bolster, with olive pits and cheese rinds tumbled round the edges. A water pipe stood near, sending acrid, sweet-smelling smoke to the ceiling. The room fell silent. Ibn Ammar clapped his hands and told everyone to go away. They grumbled but filed outside, probably to listen through the tent-walls.

The vizier pulled himself upright. He crossed unsteadily to his chair, a lovely folding chair with wide leather bands, cushioned with the fleece of a lamb. He beckoned me to sit in the next seat, a low stool. He leaned in, near to me, and touched my chin with the tip of his finger.

He smelled of sour wine and smoke.

"I am shocked. Shocked and disgusted," he said. "You are a princess of the Abadids, eldest daughter of the beautiful I'timad. On your way to marry an emir. When your father learns you were found outside in the dark with a soldier, what will he say?" He slurred the words. "Slut. How will I tell him? What do I do now? Deliver you up to the Emir with such a black mark on your honor? Will he not know that you are not the innocent maiden he was promised?"

"I do not know any soldier," I said. "I was outside the—"

He slapped me hard across the face, splitting my lip, sending blood down the front of my cloak, tearing my veil free.

"Do not speak, girl. I've heard everything I need to know already. I only need now to determine what to do—shall we let your disgrace turn us back to Sevilla, to deliver you back to your father, to somehow inform the king in Murcia that his bride was damaged in transit? Shall my first charge as ambassador be the admission that I cannot keep a little girl in her wagon?"

I decided to risk speech. "You slander me, sir. I know no soldiers. You are mistaken, Ibn Ammar. You slander me." I pinched my broken lip between my fingers, stanching the blood with the edge of my veil.

"Your own eunuch says you were out in the dark, and this soldier very near. A handsome lad."

"They are not my eunuchs, they are yours. They tell you what you want to hear," I said. "Your eunuchs slander me. You slander me. You struck me in the face. This will not stand well with my father when he hears of it."

He opened his eyes wider, trying to focus. He looked at me, considering. He poured himself a glass of wine, and handed one to me as well.

"Drink, Zaida. It is premature, but it must be done, it will be done several times before the ceremony in Murcia. I trust your mother has advised you on what to expect."

I had no idea what he meant. I told him so. He laughed, a bitter sound. "Yes, my mistake, he said. "Your mother was a slave, bought for cash off the banks of the river. How would she know the ways of imperial betrothals? And how can you be expected to comport yourself as a princess, with such low blood? It's no wonder you run loose. You cannot help yourself. A wanton, daughter of a slut." I reddened at his insults. I memorized them, so I could write an accurate account of this treachery to send to my father. The vizier picked up a little bell and made it sound.

A maid arrived, and another woman, a big woman with the arms of a laundress. They moved the lamps near to Ibn Ammar's splendid chair.

"We might as well do this now," Ibn Ammar told them.

"It will be best if you are very silent," the maid said to me.

"What are you doing?" I asked.

"Ssh. It is better for everyone if you are silent," she muttered. She glanced at the vizier, then at the big woman. She took the bloody remains of my veil and unhooked it from the remaining catch. She folded it carefully and handed it to the big woman.

"The Grand Vizier must be sure of your purity," the maid said. "It is a procedure easily done. You have only to put your foot on the seat of the chair, and I will look, and touch you very slightly, to ensure you are intact, that you've had no contact..." her face was red. Tears gathered at the corners of her eyes. "This woman is a midwife. She will attest to it. And the Vizier."

I was almost speechless. Almost.

"This is normal?" I squeaked. The woman looked again at Ibn Ammar. Then the big woman seized me by the shoulders and stuffed the folded veil into my mouth, cutting me off in mid-cry. She bore me heavily down onto the floor. She was twice my size, and knew her business. My robe was pushed up, my under-drawers pulled off, my knees forced apart. A lamp was brought down near to me, I could feel its heat. I was pinned to the carpet, and the women peered closely at the little space between my legs. One of them touched me with her finger, very gently, and I screamed almost silently.

I could not see Ibn Ammar's face, but his feet and the bottom of his robe were very near. He watched. The women finished, removed the lamp, flapped my robe down to cover me. I thought I would be allowed to rise then and get the bloody taste from my mouth, they'd seen that yes, I was a virgin, of course I was! And yes, the big woman said— "No man's been there."

And that's when Ibn Ammar's face appeared just above mine, his eyes glittering. He pushed the women aside and flipped up my robe, uncovering me again. He reached over to the remains of a plate of food, smeared his hands across it. It all went so slowly… He laid his left hand flat on the bone of my chest and leaned his weight there, crushing me flat onto the rug. He drove his greasy fingers into me below, a horrible piercing pain that made my throat close and choke. He pulled his fingers free, fumbled with his clothes, pushed down on my chest with all his weight. The cloth in my mouth, the weight on my chest… a great darkness came down as the breath was pushed from me. I expected a horrible tearing, but after some fumbling and more fingers, nothing more was done to me there. The vizier cursed, removed his weight, then stood up. He knelt again to wipe his bloody fingers on the front of my gown.

Ibn Ammar intended to ruin me, to send me home raped and ashamed—I was a weapon he could use to hurt my father and mother. But perhaps it was the wine, or the herbs burning in the pipe. Or perhaps he really did not enjoy the union of man and woman: Ibn Ammar did me a grave insult, but he did not deflower me. He could not. He was impotent.

Still, he smiled to himself, then looked at the women. "Take her home in the morning. Tell her father Ibn Ammar saved her from whoring with soldiers, where she would have met worse, but I took her myself. The poor girl's ruined. By Mu´tamid's best man! I shall send along a letter, just to be sure he knows how much we enjoyed our evening together."

He sat down at the table again, grinning, opening up a writing-chest. He gave coins to each of the women, and patted me on my cheek. "Someday you will thank me," he said. "When you begin whoring in earnest, it won't be such a shock. And soon you'll be panting after it like a bitch."

I began to cry. The ladies took me back to the wagon and Jimena, hysterical with worry.

14
SPIDERS' WEBS

I went home to Sevilla heavily veiled, riding a mule, with only a minimal guard. The two women came with us, bearing Ibn Ammar's letters. They treated me kindly, but without proper respect.

My family greeted me with haggard faces. One of my brothers was missing, my father slightly injured—they'd won a battle gloriously, but at great cost. Mu´tamid had been sequestered in his room for two days, grumbling over every dispatch as it arrived. I immediately asked for the hammam to be prepared. It was the sweetest of my life. The women scrubbed away all the skin I'd worn for the past week, and rubbed oil into the bruises. I immersed myself to my chin in water scented with jasmine. My mother came to me then, puzzled, angry. Why was I home?

I smiled my best smile but I did not rise from my bath. I told her to look in the top of my traveling trunk. It would tell my story. She left me, and there she found the gown I'd worn the night of my interview with Ibn Ammar, the greasy hand-prints, the blood. I told her what had happened, and wept into my cooling bathwater.

Mother toweled me dry, as she'd done when I was small. She saw the bruises. She put one of her thick silk robes around me, and summoned the maid and the midwife. They started out proud and just barely respectful, but they could not long withstand my mother's sharp questioning. Within moments they both swore I was a maiden still, no matter what the vizier's letter said. He had intended a great insult, but stopped short of outrage.

I was given healing broth and sent to bed, but I did not fall asleep. I could hear my father from across the courtyard, shouting and swearing. I gave myself up to weeping then. My mother spent that night with me, soothing my pain, telling me many wise things that women need to know.

My father would not see me.

His friend and vizier had apparently lost his mind.

Ibn Ammar sent word forward to Murcia that I had been found "less than pure," so the emir of course canceled the wedding. The vizier continued traveling westward, taking with him my wagon, horses, and dowry. He seemed to be on a trip of no return, and his high-handed treatment of the courtiers and troops who rode with him was rumored back home in Sevilla. The great betrayal came later, though, when he arrived at Murcia: he decked his horse with the silk flags of the royal house, taken from my wagon. He presented himself not as a humble ambassador, but as a triumphant hero, a royal personage entitled to special privilege.

It was treason, the gossips whispered to my father. The vizier's ambition had driven him mad!

The madness in Murcia, and the string of outrageous, insulting letters he sent back to Sevilla, combined to harden and finally break my father's heart. Ibn Ammar insulted the king, his father and grandfather, even my mother, calling her "Rumaik's slave, whom her master would gladly have bartered for a yearling camel, who has borne you wantons for daughters and little dwarfs that shame you for sons."

My father did not have to travel the miles to Murcia to avenge himself on Ibn Ammar—time delivered him back to us a few months later. Ibn Ammar's own soldiers rose up against him when he did not pay their wages. The vizier had to flee Murcia and wander from one court to the other, even as far as Alfonso's court in Toledo. An intrigue at Cordoba finally saw him thrown into a prison. My father had him brought in chains to Sevilla, mounted on a baggage mule between two sacks of straw. He was locked inside an old minaret tower, out on the edge of the city where the burial ground stinks to the heavens. But he still was not far enough away from the palace. He still had followers in the court. And soon the spider began again, weaving beautiful webs.

King Alfonso and the Christian army slowly moved south. He sent emissaries, Jews, to all the courts of Al Andaluz demanding gold and treasure in exchange for peace. One chilly morning a great trunk was left in our courtyard. We were commanded to return it filled with gold and silver, else our city would be burned.

The sky rained for weeks. The people fell ill. The only good news came from my brother Muhammad, missing in battle. He was alive in Jaen, fighting the Christians there.

Mu´tamid's beard turned gray. He was harangued by office-seekers and hangers-on, many of them seeking to reconcile Ibn Ammar to grace, others advising on military matters. Al-Sayyid, the sweat-smelling soldier of fortune from Castilla, offered his advice on how to outwit Alfonso. He himself had outfoxed the rich Jews of Burgos, he said, by sending them in security for a loan two trunks filled with sand and stones, giving appearance of a much greater fortune. With so many other cities sending tributes, the box from Sevilla should not draw any undue notice. Cover the box with a web of locks and steel and finely tooled leather. Alfonso never looked inside each trunk. He would never know, the wily old soldier said.

And so my father, always seeking the upper hand, played Alfonso for a fool. He had the box filled halfway with sand, and piled silver coins atop that. At the same time he sent an emissary south to Africa to appeal to Ibn Tashifin, the fanatic Almoravid, for military help against the infidel.

I do not know what was in Mu´tamid's heart during that time. He allowed me to dine with the family, but he did not speak to me. It was Ibn Ammar's beautifully written dispatch, I know… his letter had reached my father, full of lies that turned his assault into my fault and my father's humiliation.

My mother told me to be ready to go at any time, that I might have to travel some distance to marry a worthy man. It was not because of my uncertain virginity. It was because Ibn Ammar had stolen my dowry.

If any rumor circulated about my purity, it never made its way to my ears. I was looked-on with pity, as a bride robbed of her wedding rather than a ruined woman. I was mostly not looked-on at all. My troubles were minor compared to the scandal wrought by the vizier, and the threat of invasion that hung over the town. Being invisible has its advantages, and long as I veiled myself well I could move about the palace unnoticed.

It was obvious my father missed his old friend, and the counsel he'd given for more than 20 years. In the evenings Mu´tamid played his lute, and sometimes after wine he'd speak the poems of years past, and tell tales of their adventures in the darker parts of town.

Any other king would have such a traitor executed. Ibn Ammar took advantage of his hesitation, pouring forth letters of appeal, begging anyone who would listen to slip a message from him to the king. My father finally forbade the jailers to supply him with any more writing materials.

On the agreed-upon morning, gray and stormy, a great wagon rolled through our gates. It was surrounded by foot-soldiers strangely attired , Christians or Jews, I assumed— people not allowed to ride inside the city walls. I stood beneath the arches and watched the steward and his men load the great iron-bound box onto the dray. There were four more trunks like it already in the cart. I wondered how they could be told apart, and then a Jew in his a woolen robe and a round hat arrived with an answer to my query. He made a white mark on the end of the box, scribbled something on a scrap of vellum, then signaled the driver to go.

I felt my heart pound. Thunder rumbled far away, and the rain began lashing down as the gates closed behind the last of the soldiers. Their horses had left manure on the pavement; it steamed under the rain. A gardener rushed out with a bucket to collect it. Nothing is better for roses than fresh manure freshly rained-upon, the man told me.

The day was strangely warm. Black clouds dumped rain all through the day. Along the river, who can tell from where? A horse whinnied mournfully, hour after hour.

I played chess with Qamar, but she was a bad player and a worse loser. I wrapped myself in a dark robe and went spying round the palace.

In the antechambers men lounged and chattered and laughed in strange languages, throwing bones or silver blades into circles in the dirt. Messengers came and went. Mud tracked in on the tiles, the stink of wet wool and un-washed bodies drove me back toward the gardens. Rain soaked the rose blossoms into heavy, fragrant clumps. It ran in silver streams down the channels in the pavements, taking the edges off the constant mutter and hum of voices. Then something happened. The buzz of background con-versation stopped suddenly, then recommenced at a differ-ent pitch.

Something was going on. One of those messengers, maybe. News. I slipped back inside to one of several alcoves off the throne room, where the voices in the king's chamber bounced off the marble floor and into the coffered ceil-ing—sharp ears could hear every word. It was a poem, a new poem, I knew that rhythm right away! The king was declaiming a poem out loud, a most beautiful one. It was an appeal for mercy from a soul laid low, to a king brighter than the sun…

It was the poet Ibn Ammar at his brilliant best, a new composition. The king had granted him two sheets of pa-per, I soon learned—and this is what he'd produced with one of them—a masterpiece of desperate persuasion, a last appeal for a last meeting of two suffering friends.

At the poem's end Mu´tamid's voice shivered and dissolved into tears.

Tears were not a sign of weakness in my father's court. They were a show of manly sensibility. The court fell to quiet weeping, and the men outside shuffled their feet and slipped away here and there to report the new developments to their masters. They should have waited. For soon as Mu´tamid recovered himself, he turned to his scribe and ordered him to set aside an hour two days hence for an interview with the prisoner Ibn Ammar!

Some of the court burst into cheering, while others grumbled. I slipped into the wet garden, to the bower where we once made roads and bridges for the ants. I sat down there and wondered if Ibn Ammar's return to our lives would bring my father back to his old joyful self, if his advice might purge the court of low tricksters like Al-Sayyid and return us to the days of poems and music… But I was dreaming. Ibn Ammar was mad. I had seen the brute behind the mask, and I knew that man would destroy me and my family and even the kingdom of Sevilla—anything that stood between him and the king.

After our meal I was summoned formally to my parents' chamber. My mother told me to sit, and my father spoke to me for the first time in months.

It was possible, he said, that our old friend Ibn Ammar might rehabilitate himself. He would be reduced in rank and riches. If the interview went well tomorrow, and he was restored, I was to marry him within the month. Ibn Ammar could not refuse, as he'd already taken my dowry and "examined the goods," my father said, laughing at his joke, enjoying the good bargain he seemed to be striking.

"I am to marry a man who tried to rape me?" I cried, my eyes filling up with tears.

"You were not raped. Not even disgraced. The story would be much different had he done that," my mother said. "I'd have killed him with my own hands, had he raped you. He could have done much worse to you."

"He will," I said. "He called you a commoner, mother, worth a camel. And he called me a wanton. Remember? He is cruel. He's mad. He hates us."

"You don't know him at all," my father snapped. "None of this is settled. I did not want it to be a surprise, should events move to a happy conclusion. I do not want any noise from you. You are to be grateful and quiet, thankful you are not being shipped off to Baghdad! You have no idea how difficult it's been, finding a place for you."

"Soiled goods, palmed-off on the very Portuguese porter who did the soiling! And the dowry paid in advance! How convenient!" I snapped.

"We have our duties to fulfill," my mother said. Tears ran down her face.

"Leave me, child, before I lose my temper," my father said. "I do not wish to beat you. I need you to look pretty."

15
I am Chosen

I did not behave well. I went to the room I shared with my sisters, threw myself onto the pillows, and screamed like a ghost. The entire palace must have stopped and listened, then determined another of the spoiled princesses had not got things her way.

Outside the rain continued. The faraway horse whinnied in the dark, the sky grumbled and flashed, the river filled with the trunks of trees and bodies of drowned animals. When the muezzin called us to prayer, I stayed in my bed. Perhaps it was then I turned my back on Allah, back when I realized Allah, too, saw me as a camel or a mule to be traded as my father wished.

I wish I could say I behaved as an adult woman, but the thought of being married to Ibn Ammar, even a chastened, humbled Ibn Ammar, revolted me. Whilst the family was at prayer, I gathered clothing, shoes, traveling things, and put them into a coffer that a donkey could carry. I washed my face and veiled myself and went to the kitchen, where I found a crew of dripping-wet workers gathered around the table eating meat pies. The cook gave me two, knowing I had skipped my own dinner.

The men were working outside the palace walls, sluicing away the water that threatened to undermine a corner of the garden. They'd have to turn off the courtyard fountains, they may have to drain the fish pond, they said. They might as well drain the entire system, added the man with the squint: Christians don't understand fountains, and the Berbers don't approve of them. Soon there would be no need for ornamental waterworks here, or anywhere in Sevilla.

I did a shocking thing then: I spoke to them. I did not care. "Sir, is our city surrounded, then?" I asked. "I hear so many cries of "Set forth, O Andalusians, upon your journey, for it is madness to remain!," but nothing ever comes of it. It is still winter, not a good time for armies to attack cities."

The men bowed their heads over their food, embarrassed. The squinting man cleared his throat. "Lady, anyone who can find a place to run would be well-advised to do so. I have seen the Christian troops gathered in Caceres, not so far from us. They are like locusts, there are thousands of them. Their spies are everywhere in the city. Our time is short. May Allah have mercy on us, because I feel the Christians will not."

I swallowed a lump in my throat.

"And what of the Berbers, then?"

"They are still on their side of the straits, but their army is as large as Alfonso's, and they have all the conviction of true believers. I fear them more than even the Christians, because they do not want to kill us. They want to purify our souls."

"Which means they will enslave us all and seize our houses," one of them added.

I began to understand the desperate set my father's features had taken lately. Armies to the north and south, a false friend in a tower nearby and at home a screaming daughter.

"Sir, some would say you speak treason," I said.

"Lady, others would see it as reason," he rhymed back to me.

I had to laugh, as did everyone in the kitchen. The mood brightened.

"What is your name, sir?" I asked.

"I am Hamid ibn Khalikan, waterworks engineer," he said.

And that is how I met Hamid, the man who was so dear a friend to me, in the kitchen of my father's palace. He will, I pray, be remembered in San Facund for the great work he's done. The crossing of the street of the butchers is no longer a muddy, bloody bog. The water in the well near the sheep pens runs clear now, and the Jews rejoice in a sacred bathing pool of their own, with water that can be filled and drained away with the simple movement of an iron peg.

(I enjoy this writing. It is becoming easier. I am using too much ink and paper, and that is why the letters are small. The light is good here when the sky is clear. If my father could see me in these dark stone rooms, swathed in black, what would he say? Where is my father now, I wonder. And my mother?)

I return to Sevilla, where the next day was momentous indeed.

I wore an ochre-dyed dress that day, a white under-blouse, and new gold earrings. My veil was daringly sheer, but that was the fashion in those days for unmarried girls. The sun came out from behind the clouds now and then, and steam rose off the pavements. The palace was crowded with men from the south, dark-skinned, their hair oiled and their shoes strangely pointed at the toes. We were kept in our quarters, told to keep quiet. They were emissaries from Yusef Ibn Tashifin, the Berber king, meeting with father and the emirs of all the neighboring cities. We were asking the African Moors for military help, to stave off the Christians, mother said.

My brothers came for the midday meal with us, as we were having roast lamb, preferable to the couscous and camel-meat the Africans demanded. They told us how strangely the Africans spoke, how they did not understand court language or poetry or jokes. The men looked with scorn on the courtiers who sipped wine, and walked out of meetings every time a call to prayer was heard. They said the emissaries were fascinated by the marble floors, the flowers growing indoors, the velvet material of the cushions they sat on. They were like peasant children, Tariq said.

"Greedy children," Mustafa added. "Do you see how they look at the garden and the tiles? They are barbarians, unscrupulous. They cannot wait to get their hands on it all. They will come here in the name of Islam to help us, and stay on to take it for themselves."

Mustafa was always a gloomy boy, and now that he was a man he often sounded like a mullah, full of dark warnings.

He had recently earned himself a mention in the annals of Sevilla, for his advising our father against the untrustworthy desert men—to which Mu´tamid replied,

"Better a camel-driver in Africa
than a swineherd in Castilla."

My mother asked the boys how my father looked—if he smiled at all, or was pale, or red in the face.

"Father is unwell. His face is blanched white, and his lips are overly red. He is drinking," Mustafa said. "He keeps his hands inside his sleeves, so the Berber will not see them shaking."

When the emissaries left that afternoon, father did not sleep. He read and re-read the beautiful poem of Ibn Ammar. He called for musicians, but sent them away again. He took up his pen and ink pot, a beautiful, heavy glass orb, a gift from some despot in the east. My mother sent me in with a dish of dates, but he waved it away.

It was then the slave announced an urgent visitor. An emissary, he said, from Alfonso king of Castilla and Leon. I fell back with the servants, clutching my dish. My face was barely covered, so I stood behind the others, well out of sight. The room filled up with men, dusty soldiers and what appeared to be great lords, some with crosses stitched to their garments. They grumbled, as foreigners do when they arrive at the palace—they had to leave their horses at the gates, and it was a long walk from there to the palace for bodies clad in heavy mail.

From among them stepped the same man who'd come in the rain to collect the coffers of treasure. He wore the round felt hat of a Jew—a people commonly charged with carrying messages between Christians and Moors. His robes were rich and dark, his hands were clean, his beard was trimmed close to his chin. He bowed low before Mu´tamid, and in the most courtly of languages introduced himself.

He was an accountant, he said, charged with collecting and accounting for the tributes due his majesty Alfonso. He had need to inquire as to the donation made from the royal palace of Sevilla, this very place, which when opened and examined were found to be, well… irregular.

My father looked up from his table. His face indeed was pale, his eyes were strangely shiny.

"You find fault with silver and gold?"

"The king finds fault with sand and stones," the man said evenly. "Your sumptuous majesty, of all men, knows the look and feel of gold and silver. And so the shock was all the more painful to find among the greater goods of your house, more than half was of the most base element."

Father stood up, his eyes gleaming. "So I am accused in my own house, by a grasping Jew, of robbing an extortioner?" Mu´tamid's voice rose too, in anger and embarrassment. "In a transaction arranged by foul whores, I am to be the virgin?"

"You are an honorable man, King Mu´tamid. This is not in your character. This kind of low trick cannot be your doing!" the Jew cried. He spoke the truth, and my father felt the sting of his dishonor.

"Speak no more, Jew!" my father shouted. His hand grasped the great glass ink pot at his side.

"We ask only for the—the man started, but my father's arm lashed forward, and the ink pot smashed into at the poor man's forehead. It lodged into his skull, sent the man to his knees and onto his face, his blood running wide and red across the white tiles. Servants shouted. The soldiers with the man scrambled to his aid. Father's guards pulled out their swords and gathered around him. I felt sick, seeing the Jew's blood spreading out across the floor, but I could not turn away.

A man pushed himself through the crowd of Christians, a wiry man with fair hair, a trim beard, and a splendid cloak. He stepped in the blood, but did not seem to notice.

"Mu´tamid!" he shouted. My father's head looked up, with the slightest doddering. "You have murdered an upright man. You insult the kingdom of Castilla y Leon. You've brought the full force of my army down onto your own head!" His voice echoed off the ceilings.

"And who should dirty my palace with empty boasting but the infidel king himself!" my father cried. "Alfonso! What madness, to extort money from me, to speak to me so, in my house, in my city, surrounded as you are!" Mu´tamid shouted. He stepped to the wall behind his throne, where a display of beautiful weapons was hung, knives and swords from Cordoba and Toledo, symbols of old alliances. He pulled a great battle-ax from its hooks, and wielded it with expert twists of his wrist as he circled back round the dais. He strode to the edge of the blood, but did not step in it.

The northern king was not daunted. "I swear I will lay waste to your infidel dominions with warriors numerous as the hairs of my head. I will not stop until I reach the straits of Gibraltar!"

My father kept calm, and felt the edge of the ax with his fingers.

"So, king. Why not simply kill me here and now, and save your scalp the loss of all its hair?"

Both men were brave and brazen. But Alfonso was un-armed, and my father had a blade in his hand.

"Unlike the infidel, I am a man of honor. I am willing to negotiate, to speak terms, to spare lives and preserve the pride even of my enemies," the Christian said. "Had you paid the tribute agreed-upon, this murder would not be on your soul. As it is now, I expect the full price. I have earned the right to more. I want more than gold and silver."

"What more can I give you, then?" Mu´tamid said, smelling a deal. "This beautiful weapon, maybe? I believe you gave it to us years ago, as a token of your undying dedi-cation to peace. And here you are, back at my gates with an army, shouting to me about honor, and silver. What more is there, king? What do you want from me?"

"I want her," the king said. He turned and pointed his finger. He pointed at the doorway where I was standing. The people in front of me seemed to melt away. The infidel king was pointing at me. A great wave of cold washed over me. The tray in my hand clattered to the pavement.

After a very long time my father's voice was heard. "That is Zaida, my firstborn daughter. A pearl of great price. She is promised to another," he said. "You cannot expect…"

"I shall have her, or this city will be leveled to the ground," Alfonso said simply. "She is a princess, and I shall treat her as a princess. The wife I have is ill, I soon will need another. She shall have to be made a Christian."

A roar went up around us. I felt dizzy. I blinked. The maidservants gathered around me, then a wall of guards. I started to cry. I was the only one who knew they were tears of joy.

16

Betrothal Bargains

It is exciting, writing. I feel I am living this again.

I did not sleep well, I dreamed I walked through the empty palace, leaving bloody footprints behind me. The murdered Jew lay face-down around every turn, and in my hand was the big glass ink pot.

I had only two days to prepare myself, and my mother and sisters and maids did their utmost to beautify me. Father used the time to his advantage, prying from the northern king promises and amnesties. It was obvious to all he was buying time—he'd been taken by surprise, he hadn't suspected the Christians were at the very gates. He needed time to get the Berber envoys out of sight and back to the desert, where they could rally their hordes and cross back over the straits in time for the next summer's campaign.

Father dined with us at midday, in a strange, cheerful mood. His eyes glittered. He spoke about me to my mother as if I was not there. Her jewelry, he said—don't send anything too good. They don't know a cabochon from a carbuncle, all their stones are cloudy. Why not send them second-best, they'll never know. He did not give me a book of poems, a traditional gift for a royal bride. "Books are valuable. You have some of your own. Take those," he said. "They do not read or write. You may do well to keep your poetry to yourself, and your singing. They are like the Berbers that way—they have no ear for the glories of a woman's voice—beautiful things to them are evil."

Life in the north sounded perfectly horrible, but father said he was delighted at the match. This was so much better than settling for that princeling in Guadalajara, especially after what happened with Murcia, he said. I was lucky. This way I could be a queen, even if only a queen of savages.

I remembered his quip about driving camels in the desert rather than herding pigs in the north. But I suppose pig-herding is acceptable if you are a woman.

He did not mention Ibn Ammar. None of us asked him about the letter, the poem, the meeting. It stung me, my father's delight at getting full price for me, who would otherwise have had to go at a discount. But he was right—I was lucky. I would never have to share the bed of the impotent Ibn Ammar, and never again would I feel his greasy fingers on my skin. And with the wiry northern king perhaps I could have children, and know the delights some husbands supposedly provided their wives.

I was lucky another way, too. I remembered what the waterworks man had said, about smart people finding a way out of Sevilla. I ventured to speak.

"Good father, may I take along servants?" I asked, my eyes cast down.

"Of course! You must take people who can make you comfortable there, someone to cook, of course, and bake. A maid or two, healthy young ones. Your nurse. A groom, because I am sending along two Arab mares and a mule for the king's stable—the Christians are buying up every good horse in the city, paying great prices. Here I am, giving mine away." He drank down wine like it was water.

"And a waterworks man. I should like to have a fountain and a garden, and they do not have waterworks in the north," I said. "Please. We have some working here now."

"Of course! I will talk to the men myself," Mu´tamid said. I thought he lied, that he'd send the steward to sort it out. But it turned out my father did me that small favor himself. He wanted to plant a spy in Alfonso's court, and here was a chance. I was sure Hamid would seize the opportunity, and I was right.

We went to the court in full dress late that afternoon so the betrothal could be formally announced. The lamps blazed behind their precious red and yellow glass, the receiving room was like a magic cave filled with genies, fairies, and soldiers. Even a Christian priest was there, a Frank, looking dyspeptic and very far from home.

My mother had given me a syrup of poppy seeds, to make me sparkle, she said. My eyes were painted with kohl, my veil a whisp of pink silk. The world glittered that evening, the music was splendid, and the northern king was handsome in a robe of embroidered linen, soft suede shoes on his feet, his shoulders broad. He did not move his eyes from me, and so I engaged him with my glance, too. His teeth were good. His smile was ready, maybe a little boyish, even though the web of wrinkles round his eyes told me he was not young. I liked him.

The scribes called out our long, official names and titles, and I and Alfonso stood before the throne and stated our agreement. I was to begin instruction on the Christian sacraments that very evening, and would be baptized soon as it could be arranged. Within the week we would be on the Roman highway, on our way to wherever the Christian wedding would take place. And then, as promised, Alfonso the king would move his army north of Salamanca, leaving behind only client troops.

I was worth at least six months of peace.

17
FLIGHT AND MADNESS

I wish I could remember the party better. It should have been one of the best evenings of my life, it should have gone on for hours. I wore silk dyed deep red with carnelian, The poppy seeds made the colors swirl and the music and cakes and company particularly beautiful. But like so many things done in those days, the party did not go as planned.

Amid all the celebration and music a messenger slipped into the reception room. He showed my father what his old best friend Ibn Ammar had written on his second, and last, sheet of paper.

I barely noticed when he left the room. So usual, some urgent business, calling him away from a celebration. I thought little of it until I saw my mother slip away with fear on her face. I caught the eye of my sister Qamar, who simply shrugged. "Enjoy!" she mouthed to me. (That night was the last time I saw her. It makes me weep to think of her.) The Christian king was there, wearing a sky-blue tunic, he had bathed. We made a pass through the room with formally clasped hands, we danced one of the foreigners' stiff, slow dances, full of turns and curtsies. We did not speak much to one another, as the music was very loud in the closed space.

I pushed worry from my mind and enjoyed the music and poems and food. When my parents left the air seemed to leave the party, and the guests were gone before the watchmen announced the arrival of night. I changed into more sober clothes, and sat down in a chilly room with the sour-faced Christian priest to learn in two hours what it is to be a Christian. It was terribly dull. The poppy seeds made me sleepy. I sent for Jimena, who spoke the northern language—I thought she could help clarify things for me. But Jimena could not be found.

I tried to be polite, but I fear I was not attentive. Outside were shouts, slamming doors, horses ridden hard into the courtyard, then out again.

Finally the priest banged shut his book, making the waiting-ladies start out of their dozes. "Do you renounce Satan and all his wiles?" he said to me, leaning his face near to mine.

"What are wiles?" I asked him. His speech was peppered with words I did not understand, that he reeled off as if they were common usage: Righteousness. Faith. Salvation. Sacraments. Wiles. It was too much to understand in so short a time. I told him that. It seemed to make him happy, failing in his mission. He smiled a tight little smile and took himself and his book away.

I slept very well that night. Dawn was just breaking when my mother woke me. Her face was haggard, her eyes puffy with tears. She was still wearing the beautiful gown from the betrothal, but it was wrinkled and spotted.

"Take the things you need most," she said, breathless. "I will send some other things later. It will be best if you leave now. I have some soldiers to take you to the camp of the northern king." I rose from my bolster, but my mother sat down on its end and took my hand.

"Zaida, you will never be queen over those people. This king will be all you have, he will be your only protection in that place. Do everything in your power to make him love you," she said in a low, hard voice. "Learn the church things. Always be beautiful, always be clean, always be ready to receive him. Make him your friend if you can," she said. She pulled the bracelets off her wrists, removed the earrings from her ears, and tucked them inside the band of my under-trousers. "May Allah keep you, little Zaida. I love you so!" She bundled me into a woolen cape, held me close, and cried like a child. She did not follow me downstairs, as to see me away would bring bad fortune.

I know now how my mother suffered in letting me go.

Outside in the rain men waited with a pretty mule. Hamid lashed my little trunk onto the back of his saddle—I was glad I'd packed it already, back when I thought I'd have to run away from Ibn Ammar—how long ago that seemed! Out there were a cook, a groom, and a waiting lady, three servants I did not know, and Hamid. Jimena still could not be found, and leaving her behind was, at that moment, more heartbreaking to me than leaving my own mother. I choked back my tears.

We rode into the street, out over the bridge and away from the town. I did not look back.

There were many people on the road, most of them carrying burdens. Many servants and merchants were hiding with family in the countryside, Hamid told me. Something terrible had happened in the night. Rumors flew around the city, no one was sure exactly what had happened, but with help from the guards we pieced it together.

Ibn Ammar knew his final poem would touch the heart of my father, having loved and manipulated that heart for many years. Then Ibn Ammar used his final sheet of paper to seal his fate.

It was addressed to Yusef Ibn Khaldun, his closest associate in the court, one of the men who'd appealed so endlessly for Mu'tamid's mercy. It was full of boasts of what he, Ibn Ammar, would achieve once he was restored to power, what vengeance he would take. He had tricked the Christian king into retreating north, he said, so that threat was removed. He would pay off the Berbers. He would feed Mu'tamid's vanity with poems and wine and opium, while quietly taking on his powers. The sons of Mu'tamid would be sent to battle, where Ibn Ammar would ensure they died noble deaths. In the end, when the sons were gone and the king reduced to a womanish aesthete, Ibn Ammar would clap the king into a luxurious prison cell. He would take I'timad and her daughters to the slave mart and see them sold as prostitutes. He himself would step up as Emir of Sevilla, "shining with a light brighter than the sun."

What folly, to write it down!

Yusef could not keep such a potent letter to himself! As surely as if it was written on the palace wall, the contents circulated through the court, even while my betrothal was celebrated. My father, already at the end of his wits, took one look at this last testament to Ibn Ammar's arrogance, and lost his mind.

The guardsman said Mu´tamid, still in his formal finery, snatched up the Christian battle-ax from where he'd left it in the throne room. He rode to the old minaret and ran up the circle of stairs past the guards, until he stood in the little tower chamber with his old friend. Ibn Ammar, full of joy, fell at his feet. With a single mighty swing of King Alfonso's battle-ax, the grand vizier was dead.

In the following hours the many courtiers who supported Ibn Ammar scuttled out of sight. If the king was mad, who would rule? Who would be next to die at his violent hands? What army would march on the city next? Many of the servants, even some slaves, saw opportunity in the moment and ran for whatever kind of safety they could find.

And there we were, passing through the city gates, on our way to new lives. Many of the Christians of Seville were heading north. I was one of them, soon enough.

18
I am Made a New Creation

The monastery church was a cave of stone packed full of dark, dirty, people. A day's ride out of Sevilla I and my people stood alongside a heavy stone tub and had cold water poured over our heads by the dour priest. He spoke Latin, the language of Rome. We did not understand his words, but we knew this meant we were Christians. Apostates. We could not go home again.

The shock of the water on my head made me cry out. The priest removed my veil. He told me not to cover my face any more, that I no longer needed to hide, that I now lived in the light of truth. I'd have to keep my hair covered, however, to avoid becoming an occasion of sin.

Zaida, my name for 17 years, was erased. From then on I was Isabel.

Twenty-two people were made Christians with us, others headed to the Christian lands to the north. The king's French priest baptized me and my people. The rest were baptized by the local priest, a bearded monk who spoke the words in understandable language. His words had the rhythm and beauty of poems. He enjoyed his work.

At the dinner that night the same little monk slipped me a tattered, stiff little book wrapped in a soft skin.

"Please Majesty, deliver this, as you can, when you can, to San Miguel de Escalada," he said. "It is a monastery on the plains near Leon, founded by brothers from Cordoba. They fled north years ago, when the Abadid invaded and so many faithful were lost." (My great-grandfather led that invasion, but I did not tell him that.)

"This and several more books were left behind. This is the only one that is truly portable. It is old and damaged, but still readable. They will be overjoyed to see it again."

"What is it? Can I look at it?" I asked.

"By all means, Majesty," he said. "It is a psalter, a book of poems and songs written by David, the ancient king of Israel, ancestor to Our Lady. It will show you the ways of our Lord. The music is long lost, but the poetry still is beautiful. I only ask that you handle it with utmost care, and let the brothers at San Miguel know we have not forgotten our promise to deliver the rest."

Perhaps my father was wrong, I thought—Christians did have poetry and music. Apparently they borrowed theirs from Jews.

I had no idea how Jews and Christians and Islam fit together. No one ever told me until later, and even then it was in bits and pieces. Ignorance is a terrible, embarrassing thing. Parents, in their arrogance, so often keep their children ignorant of many useful things.

We stayed there for two days, while a cavalcade formed to take us north along the old Roman road. Wild stories and

rumors came up from Sevilla. Mu´tamid was on a murder-
ous rampage, they said. Then we heard the king was dead,
murdered in a tower; the princes killed, the princesses run
away, or kidnapped, or sold as slaves! I wept for my family,
knowing the truth was there somewhere. I was afraid, but
only a little. I was mostly glad to be away from the palace.

It was at that desert place I heard my first Mass, said by
the king's priest before the assembled local monks. They
stumbled through the service as if they did not know the
words. I know now why that was, and why they seemed
so frightened of the king's priest and people. I will try to
explain it. Be patient, as it is important.

Long before my people came from the African desert
to inhabit Al Andaluz, this land was a Christian place, inhabited by crude people called Visigoths. They built squat
stone churches, worshiped in their own language, chose
their own bishops and priests and abbots. Their kings and
bishops ruled from the great city of Toledo, in the center of
the land. They did not rule for long.

When the Muslims arrived from Africa, many of the
Christians ran for the mountains in the north, carrying the
bones of their saints with them. Many of those who stayed
behind converted to Islam. Others formed Christian towns
and monasteries in isolated places, or neighborhoods in the
big Muslim cities. There have always been Christians in Al
Andaluz. They soon learned that Muslims are tolerant of
Christians and Jews, people whose god is the same god as
Allah. So long as the Christians and Jews pay extra taxes
and keep to their places, all three religions lived together
in relative peace.

Things changed, though, when northern kings like Alfonso's father Ferdinand combined Castilla and Leon and Galicia into a single powerful kingdom. They began pushing the Moors south again, taking over their towns and fields, taking back what once was Christian land. The pope in Rome saw a great opportunity to increase his power. He sent his best men to Hispania, to start new monasteries, reclaim what was lost, to set up a new kingdom of God.

Alfonso reconquered Toledo, and once again it became the Christian church headquarters. All of the churches in Hispania were placed under the rule of the Bernard, the Archbishop of Toledo—our own Abbot Bernardo, from San Facund. One of the first great changes the bishop made was insisting all Christian churches, even those within the Muslim towns and cities, stop using the native Mozarabic language and rituals, and immediately change to the Latin language and Roman rites.

That is why the monks at Monasterio were so frightened when a black-robed Cluny Benedictine arrived there in a royal retinue. They were supposed to have adopted the Latin Mass years before, but in backwaters like theirs no one had bothered. They thought no one would ever know! And once the king's monks finished their stark new Mass and left for their guest quarters, the common folk gathered in to hear the old-fashioned Mozarabic service they had known for generations. I did not see much difference between the two. Both were new to me. Both went on a bit too long.

Olaya told me the old rite was still in use right there in Castilla and Leon, in the country parishes within the Benedictines' own districts. Only nobles and pilgrims and city-dwellers followed the new one, she said. (Here at our convent we use the Latin.)

The king was not there to see my conversion. He was traveling quickly north to Caceres to join with his army. His people arranged the awful two-wheeled cart for me. Hamid took it on himself to ensure I was properly cared-for. It was he who charged the groom to keep water near to my wagon, plenty of clean water.

I told you before the cart was horrible. For the first week it made me ill, or perhaps the food did that, or boredom. I tried reading the psalter the monk gave me, but I could not do so when we were moving. The days were short, we drove until the light failed, so I did not get much reading done. I was genuinely interested in what the book said, I wanted very much to learn what Christians believe. The psalms were lovely, once I puzzled-out the handwriting and old-fashioned language—cries to God for mercy or vengeance, or praises for the beauty of nature. I sometimes sang them to myself, to try to find the meter of the verses. I admit that I cried, too. Every day, for at least the first week. I was afraid and lonely.

Three days out of Sevilla my maid vanished. I woke in the morning and she was gone. She took only her own things. Hamid told Aisha the baker that she would have to take over the job, seeing as there were no cakes to bake out here on the road. She was unhappy, but had little choice.

We heard Mass each day at noon, most of it incomprehensible. I asked Aisha to ask the little nuns if one of them could explain things to me, but they all fell into giggles at the idea. From them, though, and later from Brother Rufino, I learned to pray the Rosary. They walked along behind the wagon, intoning it. It was impossible not to learn it.

We rattled along a Roman road, only partially paved. The countryside was barren, home only to scrubby oak trees and troops of half-wild pigs. One evening we camped near a crude stone sculpture, a huge black creature placed in an open plain. It was a bull, Hamid said, it was an idol, older than the Romans, older than anyone could say. The Autumn moon rose, and the creature cast a shadow even blacker than itself. Some of the women took their bed-rolls there to sleep that night. It was lucky, they said. They would have many babies, and easy childbirth.

I was still a girl. My eyes were wide and full of the new scenery, strange beliefs, the fear and excitement of the new world. I was thrilled and scared. Every day brought us nearer to the army, to the king, to the wedding. What lay beyond that I could only imagine.

19
GAMES OF CHESS

My wedding day was clear and bright. The church was newly built, dark and cold as a tomb. To the altar I wore my best dress, dyed indigo blue. I dropped my cape at the door and walked to Alfonso in only that little shell of silk. My shoes were new. My hair was dressed elaborately by a lady of that town, I was veiled in transparent green silk. I had bathed (at last!) and scented myself with lavender. My eyes were painted and my fingers and lips and the cords of my neck, as my mother had instructed, were rubbed with sand to make them sensitive to the slightest touch.

Our cavalcade met up with the king's army south of Salamanca, a muddy place just recently repopulated. It was an impressive setting, a bluff looking over a great river, spanned by a Roman bridge. Their pride was the new church of San Martin, perfectly round, made from a warm, golden stone. The rite went on and on, we stood before the altar-screen with our hands clasped as the priest droned through the scriptures. The cold soaked into my bones.

The only warmth in that place was in my hands, where Alfonso held them. He was sweating! He looked into my face through all the words and promises, and I looked into his as I made my vows. I understood the words. I was happy to agree.

Few men I had met had ever dared look me in the face. This king gave me his entire attention. Around my neck, on a fine gold chain, he hung a tiny cross. I never removed it, not until the very end.

We spent a week in Salamanca celebrating, feasting as well as we could with an army waiting on the edge of the town. Wind roared for days and nights around the house, and the stone-built room was cold, but only when I ventured from the embrace of my husband. Alfonso was not young when we married, but that only was a credit to him. Over those first days he courted me, answered my hundreds of questions, overcame my fears, won my trust. He knew how to lay a siege.

He taught me to feel comfortable without clothing. In that room I learned to move easily under his eyes, to eat and drink and play chess and other games, with my hair undone and my body exposed. At first I used my hair for a covering, to hide my breasts. I was shy about them, they were small and rather pointed, and I knew most men prefer a large, round bosom. Alfonso had me dress in every dress I'd brought. He did up the laces and buttons, then undid them again, stroking my shoulders, laying a finger along by back as the garment opened. He taught me to kiss him. It took two days. After five days I began to feel the heat he spoke of. It was afternoon, bright and almost warm. He kissed me slow and long, and we both felt it at the same time—my little breasts contracted, the nipples went rosy and stiff against his chest.

It was only then he moved in earnest. After five days of sweetness and quiet touches, he grasped and flattened his hands along the lengths of me, and made my voice catch in my throat. I was ready, he said. He stretched me out naked on the bed, and the heel of his hand opened me like a ripe fruit. So gently did he take me I felt no pain at all.

(My mother had given me a tiny knife for this, to nick a finger and make blood on the bed if there was none. I did not need the knife. For the people concerned with these things, there was blood enough to satisfy the strange demands.)

Unlike most Christians I have known, Alfonso did not see passion as a sin, but as a blessing for married men and women. And the king was responsible. Even as he slowly introduced his body to mine, he assured me that whatever children we created would be royal, fully and completely. The monks were good men, he said, they meant me no harm, that they only were uneasy with someone so beautiful, young, and unfamiliar. He was married before, he told me, but he had never met a princess who looked at him as I did, with desire. After a day or two, I enjoyed what we did. It bound me to him. I began to want him to do that with me.

I asked if our coupling was something I would need to confess to the priest. He laughed, said the priest might enjoy that, but it was no one's business what his wife did with him in his bed. He could not imagine anything so right and proper.

It was the third day after our wedding, during those hours alone in our room, Alfonso told me how he had learned of my existence. Like my own father, this king enjoyed putting on commoners' clothing and spying out strange cities. For almost two weeks before the affair of the Jew and the tributes, Alfonso and his companions had been in Sevilla. They came in with the Berbers, having told everyone they were Burgundians, looking for soldiers to fight in Zaragoza. They let their hair and beards grow and wore simple mail, nothing to distinguish themselves from the rest of the fighting men in the city.

They were there, watching, while the Jew delivered the new demand for tribute, while the trunk was dropped-off. They held quiet meetings with the courtiers in their pay. But mostly, he said, they stayed in the halls of the palace, because the floors in the rooms 'round the throne were heated.

Tanned from seven months of campaigning, and wrapped in robes and toques and djellabah there was nothing but their accents to give them away. Our court was so full of foreigners and spies that a few more strangers were not noticeable. Not even enemy kings.

It was in the court Alfonso had first seen me slinking about and eavesdropping. My clothing was too fine for a servant, and I was veiled, so not a slave. Someone told him I was the king's eldest daughter, heartsick after a broken betrothal. He looked for me thereafter, and watched me as I watched the pressure mount upon my father.

When he told me that story I laughed out loud. I never noticed the northern king. I have no memory of him before that violent day he pointed his finger at me.

"Had I known a king was watching, I would have dressed more carefully," I told him. "My father wanted me always to be clean and neat, even if I was only skulking in the hallways. I was supposed to be married within the month to a wicked old man. I had to keep up appearances."

"You would look captivating even in rags, my Isabel," he said, kissing me sweetly.

"Which wicked old man was to be here, instead of me? I know many of the men in your father's court. From which unfortunate Moor did I steal this perfect prize?"

"A Portuguese. A disgraced old poet called Ibn Ammar," I said. "My father loved him. When I was small, he was like a member of our family. But he was hateful, really."

Alfonso's face lit up with laughter. "Isabel, Ammar was a wicked man, but he was not old! He is younger than I am, and much better-looking! He would have made a better husband for a fresh young girl."

"I cannot agree, my king," I said. "He was a hateful old man. I heard he was killed, and I cannot say I mourn him." I sat up, and poured us each a cup of wine, even though I was not fond of it. Rain pounded on the roof. "Did you meet him while fighting, or making peace, or extorting gold?"

"All of those things. Several times," the king said. "Except I do not extort gold."

"That is the word used in the south," I said, smiling, "Unless of course it is my father doing the extortion. Then it is "collecting tribute."

"Smart girl," Alfonso said. "But Ibn Ammar... He was witty and cunning, a fine chess player. He was disloyal. Your father should have executed him years ago," Alfonso said. "He came to us last summer, after some debacle in Denia or Murcia, looking for a position. But in the north we have little use for discarded Grand Viziers. He did not find our weather suitable, so he helped himself to one of my best horses and headed south again. I thought he might take up with the Cid, or some other adventurer. I did not expect to see him again, and never in Sevilla."

"But you did see him. In Sevilla. Did you visit him in his prison, then?"

"Of course. The man was holding court in that little tower like an emperor. He recognized me, but called me by some other name. Wily, that one. I went only as a courtesy, and perhaps to learn a bit more about affairs at the court, and to inquire after that missing horse. For a prisoner he looked very well—his beard was trimmed, his clothes in order, and his room was hung with splendid tapestry. We took wine, had a game of chess."

"Ibn Ammar taught chess to me and my brothers when we still were very small."

"And that is why your brothers are such dangerous enemies," he said. "The game is perfect training for warriors and kings and courtiers."

"Yes. The best schemers always win. Keeping two steps ahead, or even three. We should play chess."

"In the rooms at San Facund is a beautiful chessboard," the king said. "I try to spend winters in San Facund. We will have months and months to play together, Isabel. You can teach me your Moorish tricks!"

He kissed me again, but I wiggled free of his embrace, as I still held the half-full cup in my hand. I sat it down and turned to him. The skin of my chin was chafed from his bristly beard. "So tell me, what do two men talk about over a chessboard?" I asked. "Or do you remain silent, simply contemplating the game?"

"That last time, Ammar and I talked first about the chessboard. It was splendid, made of jet and alabaster and mother-of-pearl, brought from Persia or Baghdad. God knows how he got it up those stairs. We sat down to play and made a wager—I had been drinking—that if I won, I would take the chessboard. And take back my horse."

"And if he won?"

"Like I said, I had been drinking. He did not name his stake. That was my mistake. Never play chess if you have been drinking, Isabel."

"I shall remember that," I said solemnly.

"Ibn Ammar boasted grandly through the game of the spectacular poem he'd written for the king, and how he would soon be restored to power, and how he planned to slowly take over the household of Mu'tamid. The king has taken to consuming poppy syrup—it is a wonderful treatment for wounds, but it is difficult to stop taking it. It makes a man dreamy and easily manipulated. The king would soon summon Ibn Ammar back to court, and within a day or two his plan could go into operation," Alfonso said. "It was a good, workable plan if the Berbers could be sent off. He wanted me to ally with him, to provide soldiers and financing…"

A lump had formed in my throat. Alfonso noticed how still I had become.

"Isabel?" he said.

"Oh, my father is such a fool!" I cried. A big sob came from my chest, most unattractive it was. "He was ready to restore Ibn Ammar. He was going to marry me to that snake!"

"Don't cry, girl. It ended well. It ended extraordinarily well!" Alfonso said, embracing me. "Let me finish my story. The lamp burned low, and Ibn Ammar used one of those wily tricks, and I lost the game. He kept his splendid chessboard."

"And what did he win from you?" I asked.

"He won Sevilla," Alfonso said. "His stake was the city. I was to withdraw my troops to Caceres, and leave the field clear for him to work his plan, but stay within striking distance. He thought he'd pulled a marvelous trick on me, and I thought it a great bargain, seeing as I never planned to attack Sevilla anyway—we only went to collect some tribute. So the game ended with two winners."

"And so you have your happy ending," I said. I touched him.

"The story is not finished," he said. "I learned the next day of Mu´tamid's trick, filling the tribute box with sand… so obvious, an old stunt from the Cid, from Burgos! Mu´tamid obviously was not playing his best game. He gave me the advantage. His killing of Ben-Levi was, well, unanticipated, but it only gave me more of the field. At that moment, even with that battle-ax in his hand, your father and I both knew I could name my price."

Alfonso pushed my hair off my face. "So I plucked the most beautiful jewel in the king's crown. And so the princess Zaida became Isabel. And so you became mine."

20
TRUTH

It took a very long time to move from Salamanca to San Facund. Once we left the Roman pavement the road was even worse. The carts bogged down in mud, and the landscape was an endless round of plains and trees, abandoned and lonely. I conquered the sea-sick feeling that once afflicted me, and read the psalter front to back several times. I sang every song I knew, and I learned more from others who sang as they walked or rode alongside.

I have told you what became of Aisha, the baking-maid. It was soon after that I met my first pilgrim.

He was Brother Rufino, a monk from Jerez, a tall, thin man all bristling with wild hair—he made me think of a thistle! He was from common stock, but he was well-educated in the church and its teachings.

Once the nuns were gone he took up their place in the train behind our wagons, singing the daily office and praying the rosary aloud so the rest of us could pray along with him. When we finally finished I asked him questions through the hangings of the wagon. He repeated back my questions in a loud voice, so everyone marching along could hear it, and then be "edified" by his answer and explication. His funny, clear, simple answers came in a singsong voice that was easy on the ear, softened perhaps by a lack of teeth. It was not long before he attracted notice. Good preaching is great entertainment. His exegesis on the deadly sins was especially popular.

In this question-and-answer way we circumvented the rule that barred us from speaking to one another. I could not be seen, but only heard. And our conversation was limited to matters religious. No one could object. No one did, not even the black-robed monks. In this way I could learn the creeds and commentary without any of them having to bother with me. And I learned about pilgrims.

Brother Rufino was a pilgrim on his way to the tomb of St. James at Santiago de Compostela in Galicia—Alfonso's most remote western territory. A century or two ago, a shepherd found a tomb there in the wilderness, with a great star shining to mark the spot. (How he knew the tomb belonged to one of Christ's apostles was never explained to me.) One of Alfonso's grandfathers traveled down from the Asturian mountains and had a church built there, but Almazor, the great warrior of Allah, swarmed north with his men and burned it down. Christian captives carried the bells of Santiago cathedral on their backs to Granada, where they hang to this day, oil lamps in the great mosque.

But now Alfonso is building another, greater church in its place, and Christians from everywhere are undertaking the long journey to honor the bones of Santiago. It is part of the great mission that Alfonso liked to talk about—roads, churches, monasteries, a network of towns and abbeys with San Facund at its center, funneling Christians westward to visit Santiago de Compostela, funneling money eastward to build the glory of Rome and Cluny, home of the Burgundy Benedictines.

The Benedictines preach pilgrimage to Christians all over the world as reparation for sins. They (and other holy monks and sisters) provide refreshment and rest for them at monasteries and convents all along the pilgrim highway.

And so hundreds of travelers pass through San Facund each day, heading west to the great shrine at Santiago, or heading eastward and home. They come from Lombardy, Brabant, Rome, Picardy, even Paris and Athens. Some are rich, more are poor. They bring along their songs and dances, languages, horses, and coins. All those things mix in with the local stock. Alfonso encouraged the travelers to stay and live in his lands, deserted after many years of wars. He wanted to see an empire rise, patterned after the wonders he saw in France—a civilized, cultured country that follows a higher form of Christianity. Castilla and Leon, Asturias and Galicia, even Sevilla and Granada and Toledo should be so blessed, he told me.

There is so much future in Castilla and Leon and Galicia, so many souls to benefit! The king became very noble and excited when he spoke of it.

The monks at San Facund are dedicated to this pilgrimage plan. I write harshly of them, but their motives are not completely bad. The pilgrim shelter alongside the monastery has its own cloister, and space for sixty travelers to sleep at night with a ration of bread and meat for each. Pilgrims travel together in groups, for company and safety.

They are a merry bunch. They sing and pray together, and they rob and assault one another as well. The pilgrimage is supposed to be a great religious enterprise, much like the Hajj is for my people—worshiping at the saint's shrine pays powerful benefits after death. Those who help them on their way must also be credited.

But only some of the pilgrims I saw were prayerful and pious. Others were adventurers. Perhaps Brother Rufino was one of these, a monk who grew bored of monastery life and went under cover of pilgrimage to have a look at the world. He was in no hurry to get to Compostela. He went with us all the way to San Facund, and only then joined the pilgrim trail westward. Had he cared about time spent away from his community he would have done better to stay on the Roman road northward from Sevilla, westward to Astorga. San Facund was well out of his way.

It was Brother Rufino who first explained to me about popes, cardinals, bishops, and priests. He explained the difference between the old local Mozarabic Rites and the new Latin Rites brought in from the pope in Rome. The old worship was doomed to die, he said—as a royal I needn't bother learning all its odd language and gestures. It was Brother Rufino who pointed out that my wedding was performed using the old rites. Strange, he said, for Alfonso the king had worked hard to have the new rites imposed on his territories. (At that time I could understand only a few words of either Mass. Rituals were not important to me.)

Brother Rufino stayed around San Facund for a week or two, once we arrived. Somehow I thought he would stay. I missed him once I realized he was gone. I never saw him again.

Pilgrims like to stay around San Facund. There is plenty of food for them, and places to sleep and to stable donkeys or horses. The locals view the pilgrims as people from another world, with a little whiff of holiness to them. Esteban, the holy hermit at Our Lady of the Bridge, always had several pilgrims hanging about. He put them to work mixing mortar for Hamid's building crew until they tired of honest labor and moved on to eat and sleep in someone else's house.

Most of the people who lived by Our Lady of the Bridge were pilgrims once, people too poor or sick or lazy to move further down the trail. They were pious, led in prayers by the hermit several times each day. The place was like a little monastery. I was happy to support it.

One day in autumn the wife of the sculptor arrived at our house with a basket of snails and two little boys alongside. The maids did not like me inviting inside the poor people who come to the door. They may be thieves, they said, and if something went missing the maids assumed they would be the beaten for it. But this was a woman, a person familiar to me. I had the cook take the little boys into the patio with some apples, and the woman and I sat down by the fire to talk. She was pregnant as I was, and gave me some leaves to make a herbal tea. I thanked her.

"I recognize your face," I said. "I met you before, but God knows where. Tell me who you are."

The woman giggled nervously. "Yes indeed we have met, my lady," she said. "My name is Caterina, from Badajoz. When we first met I was wearing a gray habit and white veil, walking north along the Roman road from Sevilla. One day you let me ride in your beautiful scented wagon.

It was beautiful. I felt like a princess that day. I will never forget it."

I flushed red. Caterina was the moon-faced nun, the girl whose terrible feet and endless chatter made me behave so uncharitably! She had changed so in the three years since then, it was no wonder I could not recognize her—she dressed as any poor woman, in apron and tunic, with grey-stained linen around the wrists and collar. She had gained weight, and apparently was much more happy. Her eyebrows still met above her nose, but the effect was softened by the coif of a married woman.

I was struck dumb. Caterina grinned at me while I struggled to find the right words.

"Caterina, dear God. Can you forgive me?" I stammered. "I treated you in an appalling way. I was a spoiled, stupid girl, and my rudeness cost you so dearly. I thank God you are alive."

"I've put much of that journey out of my mind now," she said. "We knew when we set out it would be an adventure. The superior who sent us north told us to expect anything. We were stupid girls, and when we found ourselves without a supervision we did not look to our prayers for discipline."

I interrupted her. "What became of your superior? I often wondered," I said.

"You wondered?" she answered. "You thought so far?"

"I am not a brute," I told her. "I don't only think of myself, Caterina."

"Forgive me, my lady," she said. "Sister Lucia was to bring us as far north as our sister house in Zamora. We paused in Merida, the town she came from, and stayed with her family. Her father was sick. Sister Lucia was not pretty, but she was of good blood. She hadn't yet made her final vows. When her father died, we suddenly found our situation changed. Sister Lucia was an heiress. If she stayed and married in Merida, the world would be at her feet. Several men expressed their interest. No one could blame her. So, after her wedding we traveled on north, accompanied by some of Lucia's father's people. They made sure we safely joined your train in Aljucén, then took our money and left us there, without even a monk to look after us. And so, in time and from hunger, we fell from our discipline. We let ourselves be led into sin. What we said to you was churlish and uncharitable. We earned punishment. We were punished."

Heaven, but that girl could talk!

We did not mention Aisha, nor did she elaborate on what had happened to her and the other nuns. It must have been unspeakable. And it remained so between us—unspoken.

"How did you come to marry the sculptor?" I asked. "Was he on that journey with us?"

"No, my lady. I arrived alone in San Facund, and the only life I knew was prayer and work—I was a foundling, raised in the convent of Badajoz. But after that journey I could never be a nun. I could not make final vows, or even present myself to be a lay sister. I was pregnant. The father could have been anyone. But I found the people at the bridge, and Brother Esteban found a place for me there."

She smiled, and I smiled. "And now you have two fine boys," I said.

"They are from God. No matter who the father is," she said, touching her belly. "But Pablo, the little one, and this one to come, they are Lucas's. The sculptor. He took me in, and we formed a partnership. He still is a kind of monk, not allowed to marry. He is kind to me and the boys, and I keep the house for him."

This sort of thing is not uncommon, she said.

"It is true I am seen as a slut in the town. But the Magdalen was a whore, and a saint nevertheless. At Our Lady of the Bridge we say as many prayers each day as I ever did in the nunnery. And at night I have a good roof to sleep under, and a strong man to keep me warm. My children will comfort me as I grow old. It is as good a life as I could ask for," she said.

We spoke of the progress at the little community, the waterworks and pavements, and the statue of Our Lady.

"Brother Esteban thinks much of you," Caterina told me. "I confess, though, I hated you, my lady, after the punishment. You and the king, too. I saw you in town now and then, and riding in style, in pretty clothes… you were pregnant too, but you were married. Everyone was so excited when you fell pregnant, but my baby was a shameful burden, a sign of my sins. And then you started coming to the bridge, being nice to everyone. I hid myself away. When the work started on the pavements and the new church, we began praying for you and the king each day. Brother Esteban said you gave up your jewels for us, but I only mumbled when your prayers were said. I was full of hatred. Lucas told me I must confess that sin and unburden my heart, or our new baby might be marked. So I did. I confessed. My heart was healed."

I found this embarrassing, overwhelming. I flushed. I put up my hand to stop her. She rattled on.

"Once I stopped hating, it was Our Lady who moved me to pray for your health and protection. I was there in the church three days ago, kneeling, and she told me to pray for you, princess. She told me you needed prayer, especially seeing the house where you live now. It is because of her I am here today."

"This house? I like this house," I told her. "It's dark and drafty, and there is no moving water. But it is a great improvement over the monastery."

Caterina looked around the room, and pulled her shawl a little closer round her shoulders.

"Do you want to know the truth?" she asked.

"Of course I do," I told her. "I hate being lied-to."

"The monks sent you to live here because they want you to die," she said simply. "This house is cursed. It is a beautiful building, but the man who built it, one of the lords of Cea, he stole the land from the rightful owners. A Basque laid a curse on the house when it still was new. Everyone who comes to live here is dead within a year. Everyone."

I felt a prickle up my neck.

"The tax collectors took the house a few years ago, because no one wanted to buy it, even for a pittance" Caterina continued. "Six priests came to pray for the spirits to leave, and to splashed holy water on the walls. The two who led the ceremony fell ill a week later, along with six more brothers and a number of people of the town. Not everyone died, but the two main priests did. I heard this from at least three different people. Women at the laundry."

Caterina kept on. "Your servants never stay here in the house with you, do they?"

"No," I said. It made sense. Deliveries were left in the doorway. Guards and messengers refused step inside to front door, even when rain was pouring down their collars. The children spent most nights at the convent, but when the nurse stayed here she insisted on sleeping in a little room above the stable. She was just across the little patio—nearby, but not in the house itself. Often as not, she took the babies there with her at night. To save them from the curse meant for me.

"What is a curse?" I asked Catherine. "I feel very well. Elvira is in perfect health, and Sancha gets bigger every day. But if you believe this place is evil, why did you risk bringing your boys here? Aren't you afraid?"

"No," she said simply. "I don't believe in curses. I think something else killed those people. Maybe they just had bad luck, or poor health. Their fear killed them. I do not think this place can hurt us, Lady. Not if we don't believe it will. We are in the hands of Our Lord, not the devil."

"It is true, He watches over us," I said. "Look at what we have survived already, Caterina. If we believe in truth, we disarm the curses."

"But the monks believe in them," Catherine said. "They are sure you will die here, and maybe your little ones too. They hope you will. Because they have other plans that everyone knows, but I am sure no one has told you. Not even your man Hamid."

Now I felt truly frightened. My eyes filled up with tears. "I am not sure I want to hear any more truth today!" I told her, half-seriously. "How does the wife of the sculptor know more of the king's plans than the wife of the king knows?"

"The Camino de Santiago passes my door," Catherine said. "Everyone stops to see the new chapel and critique Lucas's work. They talk. They have seen and heard in the days past the news that is coming our way, down the trail from the east."

And so the river people heard the news before anyone else in town, except for private messages that heralds and horsemen carried. And that is how everyone but me knew the monks of Cluny had found a new bride for the king. She was 15 years old, from Lombardy, deeply pious and remarkably well-educated. She would not live at San Facund, but in Leon, with a proper court, as a proper queen. Her name was Berta.

On their way to Leon and the coronation the royal couple would stop in Pamplona, Logroño, Burgos, and Carrion de los Condes. If the cold weather held off, they could be in San Facund by Christmas.

21
HOUSE OF DEATH

Catarina's truth brought me back to earth. I did not know what fate the king had chosen for me, or what the monks had in their dark minds. I had become an obstacle. My easy life in the Death House could not continue. I lived in a place that admitted no long-term tenants.

Since I was slated to die or disappear, I took steps to lay hold of what life remained to me.

I adopted Caterina's practical thinking as to the house. I do not believe a building has powers to kill its inhabitants, unless some noxious vapor or poison is introduced there from outside. I think the monks felt the same. They preyed on the fears of others.

The fault in the monks' plan was assuming I knew about the curse and believed in its power. In my ignorance I flourished there, me and my babies with me. If someone had told me earlier, would I have believed, and then died? I do not know. I come from a superstitious people. I did not like the house at first, but it had become a joyful place.

For a little while I fantasized the monks' frustration at the very things that brought me joy: the little church on the river growing taller by the day, Elvira and Sancha with such rosy cheeks, and the king getting still another healthy child on his Moorish whore. How it must grate on them, every time they see me! I thought.

But reality returned in time. It was clear the abbot did not believe in curses. I was given the house because he wanted me out of the royal apartments, and the Death House was the best option. It cost him nothing. I was near enough to keep an eye on, but far enough away to not be bothersome.

I also realized how absorbed I was in my own state. I spent hours wondering what the abbot and prior and monks were thinking, what their plans were for me and my children. I felt hated and conspired-against, until I considered all the machinations of Alfonso's wars, and the Cluny monks'great network of religious houses, and all the accounts and concerns of the great monastery and town of San Facund. I realized my presence there was not a great concern, not to the king nor the abbot. I was a detail, an annoyance.

Hatred requires a great deal of energy, and Abbot Bernardo would not waste such energy on my small soul. I was only another problem, to be dealt-with in due time. I was not so important.

I was humbled. I could see no future for myself, so I stopped thinking of any future beyond the birth of my new child. I was sure it was a son.

I rediscovered the little Psalter I used on the road from Sevilla. I had meant to give it to Alfonso, to be delivered, as promised, to the monastery near Leon. I was happy I had delayed, though, for in those days I re-discovered the poetry of David the King. He, too, struggled against powerful enemies. He too called on God to save and vindicate him—and he wrote it out as poetry:

> *"For your servant David's sake,*
> *do not turn away your face,*
> *The Lord has sworn an oath to David;*
> *in truth he will not break it:*
> *"A son, the fruit of your body*
> *will I set upon your throne.*
> *If your children keep my covenant*
> *and my testimonies that I shall teach them,*
> *their children will sit on your throne for evermore."*

It is likely I violated some law by possessing that holy book and reading it—me a Moor, a woman who is not a nun. And to interpret it without a priest to tell me what it means? I did those things with perfect delight, because the Lord himself put the book into my hands. It was a soothing balm for my troubled heart.

The days were long, and I was bored and lonely. When Olaya visited I asked her what was said by the women at the laundry-pool. Gossip is always entertaining!

And so it was confirmed: I was moved from the royal apartments so they could be made-over. Not for the abbot, but for the new queen. Once she produced children, she would move to San Facund. She would sleep in the bed where my babies were born. She would hear the fountain splash that I had installed in the cloister garden. Perhaps she would wash in the water kept hot above the kitchen fire.

Perhaps she would wash, I chuckled to myself.

This was the most grievous to me—to know another woman would reap what I had sown, and enjoy the very luxuries I brought to that place. Like Ines, the princess who brought the fruit trees to the cloister—I thought of her when I tasted the apples from her trees. Would Berta think of the Moorish princess when she washed her white face and tiny hands, and saw the doves cooing and splashing in the courtyard fountain?

I knew the abbot coveted my carpets, as Sister Ana had duly reported them. The maid at the Death House that summer took their measures and described them in detail for the monastery steward (as well as her friends at the washing pool), along with descriptions of most of my household goods. The guard, maid, and cook reported my visits and visitors, and overheard what they could of what was said in my house. The abbey paid them in bread.

I look back at this, and see my heart was broken then, but in a cold and passionless way. I did not take meat or wine, for fear of poison. I did not much care if they killed me, and they might have done if not for the baby that leapt and danced inside me. They, too, were sure it was a son.

It was then I began mourning, even before I lost anything. I did not know what would become of me, but I knew my life was coming to an end. I knew I would lose my children.

I cried, jealous of the women who would hold and nurse them in years to come, heartbroken at the pain my Elvira and Sancha would feel when I was no longer there for them. I cried for my loss, and I cried for my children's loss, too—for what would they know of their mother? How would they know how much I'd loved them? Would they be ashamed of their dark skin, taunted for their "impure blood?" What kind of lies would they be told about me, and about my parents, and Sevilla, and Islam? After a few years, would my babies remember me at all?

The king promised from the start that my babies would be princes and princesses, his own children, heirs to his kingdom. But Alfonso lied about other things. I prayed to Our Lady that this was not a lie, too. That even if he and the monks put another woman in my place, he would not set aside his own flesh and blood.

But he would. He had. My tender husband was a cold-blooded ruler.

Castilla y Leon ruled over great reaches of Hispania because Alfonso would not share his father's kingdom with his brothers Sancho and Garcia. By brute force and trickery, and some people say murder, Alfonso defeated them both and united the kingdom. He ruled over lands and people, and he ruled over religion, too. Archabbot Hugh of Cluny was the uncle of Alfonso's second wife, Constanza. She leaned on the king to clean up Hispania's ragged old Mozarabic monks and rituals and replace them with Benedictines and their Latin worship. The Christians in the churches resisted, of course. So Alfonso put God to the test.

(He told me about this himself. It was still a little embarrassing to admit, but he was still a young soldier then. One must forgive him some childishness.) On Holy Week of the year 1077 in Burgos, Alfonso the king declared a Trial by Duel, wherein he had two warriors evenly matched and armed. One he labeled "Rome." The other represented the old liturgy. The two of them battled for hours, with spears, swords, maces, clubs. They put on a great show, and in the end, Rome fell down exhausted.

Alfonso demanded more proof. He had two bulls put into a ring, named one Rome, and set dogs on them, to enrage the bulls enough to turn on one another. The bulls fell together, with no clear victor.

So finally, in the great city of Toledo, Alfonso took two great books, one of the Roman ritual, the other of the Mozarabic, both beautifully made. He had a great fire kindled, and threw both books into the center of the blaze. The Roman book was consumed. The Mozarab book leaped out and spun across the floor. The king kicked it back into the flames.

Somehow, even with all this "evidence" to the contrary, Alfonso declared the Mozarabic must be put aside, and the Roman rite should be imposed. It is the stuff of legend now, and a saying of "God makes laws, but the king decides if they apply."

Latin or Mozarabic, prayers turned to babble to my ears. The same priests who brought the new and improved Latin also dictated when and how common people should eat and drink, sleep and work. They taxed the peoples' homes and food, and plucked away their most promising children to become monks and nuns. The king ceded too much power to his servant the abbot, and the abbot became a tyrant. Our Lord Christ warned us of these things in his parables.

My father Mu´tamid said Christians were savages. I sometimes thought they were mad. Perhaps I was driven mad by them for a time. But now that I am old, I know it was not the monks of San Facund who drove me to despair, nor was it my husband the king.

It was the winter fog, and loneliness, and wondering what would happen to my children once their mother was gone.

22
I Am Summoned

The days grew short, the mornings misty. My belly grew round. Yasmin the midwife said the child was in perfect health.

Olaya learned she would have a baby too, in the summer. On the day of Christ's Nativity she and Hamid celebrated with a noisy feast. I left early, I tired quickly. Hamid accompanied me to my door. (He never entered the House of Death himself, I noticed!) Before I went inside, Hamid made a formal bow, announcing something serious was going to be said. "I made a promise to your father, our king Mu´tamid Ibn Abadid, before I left Sevilla," he whispered, "and I will keep my word. I told him I will keep Zaida safe if she will let me. I pray you will let me, Zaida," he said.

Fear rolled over me. "What is happening, Hamid?"

"Zaida, the king arrived today in Carrion de los Condes. He will be here within the month."

I swallowed hard, and wished I had not eaten the oily pastry. "The signs in the sky to foretell great and terrible change, for us and for Al Andaluz," Hamid said. "Keep your doors bolted. I think no harm will come to you long as the babe is unborn, but trust no one," he said. "I'm sending a cart tomorrow. You need to send what remains of your valuables from this house, before someone devises a way to take them from you."

The following narrative was written the next evening, in an effort to make sense of the events of the day. I will copy it out for you:

> I sat this morning saying my rosary before the fire, and who arrived at the door but Sister Ana, the buzzard who used to spy on me when I lived at the palace. She usually is kept indoors, so I knew this visit was important. She was flushed and nervous. I had her sit. And cruelly, piously I had her finish praying my rosary with me—almost three decades.

> Afterward we had cakes, and I sent the maid away from the door where she was eavesdropping, Sister Ana told me I was expected at the monastery after the midday Mass. Come to the chapter house, she said. Important news has arrived for you.

> She said no more. She almost fell over her robes, getting away from me and from the Death House! By then Nones was not far away. I washed my face and hands in water and lemon-peels, had my hair wound under my coif, put my cape over my big body. I would not ordinarily go out now that I am so big, but in this town, when commanded by the abbot even I must go.

They did not expect me at the Mass. A mumbling went up at my arrival. I could not navigate the narrow stairs to the gallery, so I sat where visiting nobles sit, to the right of the altar. The great Abbot Bernard was there in his grand seat behind the altar, but he pretended not to see me. I kept my head up, said all the responses at the right times.

And when the holy host was consecrated I moved forward to accept the Body of Christ in the form of the bread. I opened my mouth like a baby bird before the priest, where he stood with the sacrament in his fingers. He only looked down at me from his great height. His eyes cut toward the abbot, as did mine. The abbot was not looking at us. The bread was poised in the priest's fingers (his fingernails had dark moons of dirt beneath them). He was not putting the bread on my tongue. He was refusing me the only spiritual food I had ever received in that cold place.

So my hand shot up to his, and took the little bit of bread from it. I put it into my own mouth.

I went back to my seat. I did not look at the priest again, my face was so red, my eyes filled up with tears of fury. The Mass went on with a great clatter of the sacred cups and saucers.

I was strengthened by the sacrament. I could feel the Holy Spirit coursing through my body, pounding in my temples and my wrists and in the tips of my fingers. God was with me, even if I had to seize him in my hands and teeth. I stayed in my seat with my head down until the singing ended and the church emptied. I gave them time to go to the chapter house and make things ready.

They sent a boy for me, a little monk just newly shaven. He was afraid, too. He held my hand as we walked across the beautiful garden, and I dipped the fingers of my other hand in the fountain-bowl as we passed. The doves cried to one another. I breathed deeply, and stepped inside.

The chapter house is beautiful; I had never seen it before. It is built by Arabs, with the sort of brick made in the south—the dome overhead was brick, too, and would better suit a church. It is here the monks gather to confess their sins to one another, to make decisions and hear decrees, to accuse and to judge. Benches lined the walls on three sides, and every place was filled. The abbot's great chair faced them. Prior Martin sat behind a table-full of scrolls and books, his pen at the ready.

They all were there, sitting, every monk I ever saw about the place—even the bakers, their habits and chins dusted with flour, and the stable boys, smelling of horses. I stood before the abbot's table and turned to face them. They all, as one, looked down their noses at me.

I was not cowed. I concentrated on a straw on the bottom of a scribe's shoe, stuck there with manure. The abbot entered, they rose. He intoned a long, windy prayer, and all of them sat again. No one offered me a chair. I turned to face the abbot, who was busying himself with the things on his table. The torches were damp and guttering. The dome overhead filled slowly with the smoke.

I inclined my head to him.

"You summoned me, abbot." I said.

"We did." he snapped. He sat back in his chair and sighed.

"Isabel of Denia. The king directs us to inform you of your standing here at the priory of San Facundo and Primitivo, the church of San Mancio, as well as town of San Facund the kingdom of Castilla and Leon." I nodded. He picked up a paper and cleared his throat. (I copy this from the document itself):

CONFESSED:

"For his own reasons, and against the advice of God and man, Alfonso the king, at the time widowed, brought Isabel, then known as Zaida bint Abadid, from the infidel city of Sevilla to the church of Monasterio in the Taifa of Sevilla, where after sufficient instruction

Zaida was baptized a Christian, using the rite elected by the Holy Father of Rome, as administered by our brother Johann of Mainz, even now traveling as the king's confessor. The infidel princess Zaida took the name Isabel, in memory of the mother of St. John the Baptist and cousin of the Most Blessed Virgin. Our brother Johann testified even before the baptism of the woman's utter ignorance of the tenets of the Christian faith, but her willingness to receive the sacrament of baptism."

"Isabel then received instruction from a pilgrim monk of the Augustinians of Jerez, who also taught her Psalms and proverbs. And upon arrival in Salamanca, after meeting the train of the Alfonso the king, for his own reasons and against the advice of God and man, did contract with Isabel a matrimonial agreement. An unlawful and uncanonical ceremony was performed, before witnesses, at the Parish Church of St. Martin of Tours. From that point Isabel did continue to cohabit with Alfonso the King , in a state of concubinage. Isabel styled herself queen, and robed herself as such, and referred to herself as such in the hearing of others, thus being caused by the king himself to commit treason against the throne and sow scandal among the faithful.

"The king did, for three years, keep the woman at the royal apartments of San Facund. For his own reasons and against the word of God and counsel of man he *did cohabit and behave in every way as a man does with a legal and sacramental wife, providing Isabel with servants and apartments, violating the laws of descent and concupiscence which mitigate against the elevation of infidels to the roles of Christian courtiers. He did, against the word of God and counsel of man, get on her two children, known as Elvira and Sancha, both declared true daughters of the house of Castilla and Leon. The woman now is great with another child, supposedly of the king's seed. The king Alfonso does not deny these facts, and declares himself the father of all the children born of Isabel of Denia.*

His majesty the King Alfonso, emperor of all Spain, does hereby confess to the following sins commited with and against the Moor Zaida, also known as Isabel of Denia:

Rebellion against the word of God and counsel of man; Lust.
Concupiscence.
Adultery. Causing another to commit adultery.
Unclean and unnatural deeds in the execution of marital duty.
Violation of the sacrament of marriage.
Contracting marriage using rites uncanonical and barbaric.
Bearing false witness, creating false contracts.
Causing another to utter treason.
Mixing the royal blood with unclean races.

Creating children of impure and mixed race.
Submission to enchantment or sorcery.
Rebellion against the Divine Will.

I confess my sins before the Lord and you my brothers,
and I pray for God's mercy upon my soul, and for His
continued kindness to Isabel of Denia, who I ask to be
set aside and cared-for among the Benedictine sisters
of San Pedro de las Dueñas as soon as possible after the
delivery of her child.

Should she not survive the delivery of her child, I
command and set aside a weekly provision of bread
and wine for 13 pilgrims at the pilgrim hostel of San
Facund, who in exchange shall pray for the repose of
the soul of Isabel of Denia, following the practice es-
tablished for the souls of queens Ines and Constanza,
the king's late spouses. Isabel's body shall be interred in
the monastery of San Facundo with those of the king's
legitimate wives."

The king had signed and sealed the document. I was
given a copy, in the Carolingian script. I stood silent
for a moment. I was supposed to say something.

"I do not understand the language," I said.
"Uncanonical. Concubinage. Please explain."

"*It means that we warned the king from the start that he should leave you among your own people. That bringing you here was wrong,*" the abbot said. He spoke softly, matter-of-factly. His voice filled the room. The monks leaned in to hear better.

"*It means that the wedding performed in Salamanca was of the old Mozarabic rite, which the king himself set aside 16 years ago in favor of the correct Roman rite. Your baptism was done in the Roman rite. You are a Christian. But your marriage is invalid. You are not the king's wife. You are not our queen. Your children are bastards, and as such are not legitimate heirs in the royal line. The king, however, in his kindness has named them as his own, and they will be educated and provided-for.*"

"*You are taking my children from me.*"

"*Your children will be educated and provided-for,*" he said. "*By the king. No mother could ask anything more for her children.*"

I tried to keep my dignified stance. I tried not to feel faint. A lump rose in my throat that I could not fight down. My voice shook when I finally said,

"*And I am to be a nun.*"

"No," the abbot said. "A mother of children, and her husband still living? No."

"I do not have a husband," I said. "You just told me that. My wedding was a lie."

"Well then, a mother of two children who has no husband surely cannot take the vows of a bride of Christ, can she?" An ugly edge entered his calm. "You can stay at the convent, just not as a choir sister. Your possessions will be forfeit. Your friend Sister Ana de Leon is superior there. She will help you adjust. You can write, and sew, and read. You can illuminate psalters, perhaps."

"Yes. Psalters. Psalms," I said. "A Psalm. Number 62. Surely you know this Psalm, father?"

And something came over me, the Holy Spirit, or the spirit of my father the poet. I turned toward the assembled monks and recited it in the style of the Moors, moving side to side, using my hands and turning my head. It is a beautiful poem:

For God alone my soul in silence waits;
*   from Him comes my salvation.*
He alone is my rock and my salvation,
*   my stronghold, so that I shall not be shaken.*
How long will you assail me to crush me,
*   all of you together,*

as if you were a leaning fence, a toppling wall?
You seek only to bring me down from my place of honor;
lies are your chief delight.
You bless with your lips
but in your heart you curse.

For God alone my soul in silence waits;
truly my hope is in Him.
He alone is my rock and my salvation,
my stronghold, so that I shall not be shaken.

Steadfast love is yours, O Lord,
for you repay everyone according to his deeds."

At the end I folded my hands and bowed my head.

"Moor, how dare you prate holy scripture in low
language?" I heard the abbot's voice behind me.
"Unworthily you snatch the very body of Our Lord
from his priest. Unworthily you turn holy scripture
to cheap entertainment. Unworthy you've been found,
it is clear to all. You are a scandal and a curse. Now
go back to your accursed house, and give birth to that
wretched child. Go now. We have work to finish here.
The king will be here soon. With his queen."

And so I went. They will not see me again.

23
Divine Will

I thought I would have a son to show the king when he finally came back to San Facund, but the baby waited. It was a cold, wet January. I spent my days telling stories and singing songs to Elvira and little Sancha, hoping they would somehow remember some of them—southern stories of magic lamps and enchanted gardens. It was hard not to teach them distrust and spite. I was full of anger and bitterness, disgusted with people who spoke of nobility and honor and glory with blackened teeth and dirty hands and shit stuck to their boots.

We waited. The monastery was scrubbed and decorated, and dozens of hogs were butchered for the feasts to come—their screams could be heard all over town. At my house Olaya and Hamid kept me supplied with cabbages and kale, firewood and dried fish. I lived like a nun in bare rooms, as I had moved most of my things to their safekeeping. I gave away trinkets and clothing to Olaya and the servants, toys to the children at the bridge. The little bed with the angel-faces I gave to Caterina, for her children had no beds at all.

The sisters would expect a dowry when they took me in, but no mention had been made of how much, or if the king would pay it. I pondered long on my past, and on my children's futures, but I did not consider what would become of me. I could only think of the baby's birth. After that I could envision no kind of life at all.

Finally one icy morning a knock was heard at my door. It was Alfonso the king, unannounced. He had slipped early into town, he said—he wanted to speak to me before all the formal festivities began. He stammered like a boy, and smelled of sweat and sour wine. I did not rise when he entered the room. I stayed in my chair by the fire. Rising was difficult for me.

"I heard your confession," I told him. "The abbot read it to me, in front of a gallery of keenly interested monks. You lied to me. You made a great fool of me. And the abbot made a fool of you."

"I made a fool of myself," he said. "No one can be blamed but me."

"All will be forgotten, soon as the baby comes. I will be shuffled off to the nunnery, swept out like last year's rushes. If the baby is a boy, your fresh new princess will be relieved of providing you an heir. But then again, if you want one that is not a half-blood bastard, she may have to sacrifice her girlish body."

I thought he might strike me, but the anger moved over him quickly. He sat down on the little stool near the hearth, his sword crossed over his knees. In the light I could see the deep lines around his eyes and mouth, and the grey in his whiskers. He was growing old—he was probably more than 50. I almost felt sorry for him.

Then he looked me in the face.

"I didn't go to Sevilla looking for a wife. I always just took the ones provided for me. I have never been much interested in wives, except for when I was a boy."

I cocked an eyebrow at him. "What made you change your mind?"

"You did. Watching you glide around that palace in your little red shoes. You were interested in everything around you. You eavesdropped, you watched the men laying pipes in the garden, you heard the arguments in your father's court, and you tasted every bit of food on your plate. You were so lively, and so sad, too—you were a princess, someone I thought was attainable. And you were beautiful."

"Thank you," I said. "You must then excuse my present appearance. Events have intervened."

He laughed, just for a moment. It was good to see him smile. I let myself smile a bit too. Just for a moment.

"I was angry at the time, and sad, too—Constanza was dying. I thought it would make political sense, marrying a daughter of Sevilla. I knew your father would be happy with the idea," he said. "You were a princess, a noble. Marriageable. I wanted you. I'd never seen anyone quite like you. I wanted to know you, and have you. So I took you with me."

"Well, then. So you did," I said. "You lied to me, for years. All this time I thought I was your wife, the consort, the mother of the princess, maybe not quite a queen. But your confession says I am your concubine. A Moorish whore. One cut above a slave. Everyone knew but me. Why didn't you tell me, Alfonso? I could have learned to live with that, I think. But you let me live on like this, thinking I was your wife, a fool before the whole world."

"I did it because you are a princess. You deserve to live as a princess."

"Why did you marry me in Salamanca in some false way, if you could have married me properly? You are the king. Can't a king do what he likes?"

He sat back on his little stool. "No," he said. "I cannot. Because I am the king, I cannot do everything as I want. Otherwise this terrible thing would never have happened to you, Isabel. If I could do what I wanted we would live in the great palace together in Toledo, or in Sevilla, near to your family. Or even Leon. You would have been crowned queen soon as we arrived there—Leon is the center of the kingdom."

"So why here, in this place full of hateful people? Why not Leon?"

"You had to live here, where the abbot could, well… It's important that the community of Cluny remain in close contact with my children, my wives. My wives have always come here to live."

"And to die." I felt my tears begin to fall.

"Isabel. I am trying to explain myself. Please."

"So tell me then. Why does a priest in Burgundy control the emperor of all Hispania?"

Alfonso rose and crossed to the kitchen door. He told the servant girl and cook to take Elvira and Sancha to the monastery kitchen—he had no interest in seeing the girls right away. They would be warm there, he said, and well-fed. When they left he returned to his place by the fire.

"Archabbot Hugh of Cluny is a saint," he said. "He is bringing the world together under one kind of Christianity, the way Christ himself wants it to be, the way the prophets predicted. Kings like me, and the kings in England and Aragon, are working with him to bring the kingdom of God to earth. Archabbot Hugh has a vision—a comprehensive, beautiful, sweeping vision. Making it reality means lords of the earth must bend their will to the Lord himself. The ways of God are not always the ways of man," Alfonso said. "My father was first to see the sense of it, and my mother. And I have followed."

"I have heard all this before, several times," I told him. "Visions. Latin rites. His Holiness the Pope and Archabbot Hugh, boyhood friends. I do not know what they are, but they want to take everything from me."

"I am the king, but I'm still just a man," Alfonso continued, as if I had not interrupted. He stared into the fire, he did not look at me. "I rebelled against God's will. That was why I had to write that confession. I have been forgiven for those sins, but the earthly penalty still must be paid."

"By me. And by Sancha and Elvira," I said flatly. "And this baby, too."

"None of us can stand in the way of divine will," the king told me, looking very noble in the firelight. I drew in a great breath.

"So it is God's will that my children be taken from me, and I spend my life shut away in a convent?" I said, a bit too loudly. "Is it God who says I am a whore, and our babies are bastards? Why did God accept my baptism, but not my marriage? Are not they both sacraments? Can a Moor take only one, and not the other? Does God despise people with dark skin, as the monks do? Did not God himself create me with dark skin?"

"Isabel, it is not God's will that makes it so. It is sin. It is not God who treats you badly. It is man. Sinful man."

"Your monks, then, and I daresay your Archabbot Hugh, are sinful men," I spat at him. "They would bless our marriage on one hand, and break it apart when it suits them. Your archabbot has never set eyes on me, but he despises me to the point of denying me Christian sacraments."

"It is not a matter of your person, Isabel. It is his sense of purity. Your bloodline is impure. Your dark skin is an outcome of the darkness of the infidel race, the sins of all your forefathers who lived without the divine light of Christ. In baptism your own soul was shriven and made clean. But your seed still is cursed. It should not be mixed with the pure blood of a Christian king."

"And why is Archabbot Hugh of Cluny so concerned about the bloodline of Leon and Castile?"

The king leaned close to me. He motioned me to lean in to him. I did as well as I could. The baby kicked. The king spoke quietly.

"Archabbot Hugh of Cluny is concerned about my bloodline because he considers it his bloodline. Archabbot Hugh is as good as my father," he said quietly. "He loved me best of all my brothers. It was him who sent me to live with righteous men, to be raised up a warrior of Christ. I think he intended me for the church, but I am a passionate man, unfit for that life. You know that, dear Isabel, maybe better than anyone."

He touched my cheek with the back of his hand. I pulled away.

"So what about your brothers? Wasn't Sancho the eldest? What became of him, if you did not have him killed? And your younger brother, Garcia, the prisoner in the castle?"

"Christ, Isabel. No one should ask me these things," Alfonso said, his jaw tightening. "Nobody would dare. You are a brave girl. Maybe a stupid one."

"I'm as good as dead. I have nothing to lose. Neither do you. Tell me," I said, my voice flat.

"A pure and single Roman Catholic world will be the legacy of Hugh of Cluny, with all of Hispania as its stronghold and Saint James as its patron." He sat up straight for a moment, then let his chest deflate. The stool was low, not the best platform for posturing. The hour was early, and the bags beneath his eyes colored dark. I sat quietly.

He recommenced in lower tones. "My father Fernando was king of Leon and Asturias, the ancient royal line. He fell under the spell of the great Hugh of Cluny, and his wars financed the great monastery up there, far in the north. His wars, and later mine. We sent the silver wrung from old Al Andaluz, carted it right over the Pyrenees mountains. Old Hugh is a charismatic man, persuasive, I have never met his like. My father was a great warrior and Christian, but like me, my father rebelled against the abbot's hard rule. When he died, my father's will undid all his own hard work. The kingdoms my father fought hard to unite: Castilla, Leon, and Galicia, were parceled-out between me and my two brothers. He charged us all to live together like Christians. But of course we had to fight his wars all over again, among ourselves!"

"No, you didn't," I said. "You all were Christians, no? Why couldn't you all have done as he asked, and each ruled your own kingdoms in peace?"

"Stupid girl. It was the fault of your people, the god-damned Muslims—they do not understand what peace is. They never settle down within their borders. And my god-damned brother Sancho, who always wanted everything for himself. He almost took it away from me—it was a close-run thing, Isabel. I almost ended up as a monk my-self, right here at San Facund—I hid in Toledo, then tried monastic life for a little while, and found it most absurd. My brother grew bored and moved west to overrun my sisters in their cities. Urraca sent word from Zamora, she needed my help. Then my luck changed."

"Sancho was killed outside the walls of Zamora," I said.

"I swear before the throne of Christ I did not kill him," Alfonso said. "But he had to die. He was a a victim of treach-ery." I said nothing, so he continued. "Only Urraca knows what happened there. And maybe Archabbot Hugh."

He saw my look of puzzlement. "Urraca is my sister. Zamora, the city, was her birthright. Sancho tried to take it from her, and he died in so doing. My daughter Urraca is named for my sister. The Muhammadans think she was my lover," he said, shaking his head, smiling. "They know nothing beyond carnal love, the Moors."

"And you know so much more of love than we do," I said.

"I mean no insult to you personally," Alfonso said. "You are an exceptional woman. As a princess and as a Christian, you must understand. Archabbot Hugh understood. Sancho had to die. Garcia had to be moved aside—he was weak, effeminate. We need a strong ruler in Galicia, in Portugal, right there up against the Moors!"

I took a big breath and let it out. The baby's foot traveled the width of my belly, from hipbone to hipbone. I wondered if his father could see the little wave moving across my girth.

"It was all about the kingdom of Christ on earth, fulfilling the prophecies of St. John, bringing about the fulness of Scripture," Alfonso said. "It the work of God, bigger than any of us. And for that same reason the archabbot chooses pure Christian maidens to be wives for me, noble women of near relation. That is why the monks were thunderstruck at my choosing a princess of my own, and a Saracen at that! Little Elvira and Sancha, and the babe to come? They are heirs to the vision of Hugh of Cluny, but imperfect. To him, the thought of pure Christian blood in the veins of Africans and Arabs? It is heresy. He must—I must—have a son of pure and noble blood, a prince who is white and pure and Christian, to continue the work."

"So you and I and Berta the new queen are only stallions and mares on the stud-farm of an old celibate," I said with a sigh. "Constanza the queen, and her cousin Ines…near relations to the archabbot. Pure-bloods. Thoroughbreds."

Alfonso shrugged his shoulders. "The bottom-most truth is, the archabbot is a good friend to His Holiness Pope Gregory. There is no opposing them, Isabel. Not even a king can do it for long."

I sat back in silence for a moment. Alfonso put a stick of wood in the fire.

"I opposed them once before. Her name was Ximena. She was witty, a brilliant woman, another chess-player," he smiled at the memory. "She gave me girls, too—Teresa, and another little Elvira. I claimed them as mine, but only as bastards. I set them up in their own house, and noble matches are made for both girls."

"And why did you not marry her?"

"She was already married, Isabel. So was I. Eventually the word traveled. The priests made my life impossible, and then my men, my army, started to fall apart. They deserted, they fell sick. I lost too many good men that year—your father led one of those bloodbath battles... Plague broke out in Burgos, and dysentery. My best friend died at my side. The Lord turned his face from me, and the reason was clear. I repented, did a public penance. I settled some money on Ximena and the girls. I left them."

"So I am not the only one, then. How comforting," I said bitterly.

"I hated them for taking her from me," Alfonso broke in. "I was manipulated. Then Constanza grew sick and querulous, and so very pious. I left to gather tribute from Badajoz, and from your father in Sevilla. She died soon after. Then I saw you. A Moor, but a princess, a princess of my choosing, and then a Christian. I brought you back, and I put you here, right inside the abbot's house, so they all could see who is king. I rubbed you into their faces. I didn't consider how they would treat you. And you did not complain to me."

"I complained to you on the road from Sevilla, and saw what happened," I told him. "Two people horse-whipped, and a group of girls sent to a life of misery. So I was afraid to complain, afraid to ask questions. Even when I learned our wedding was done in the old rite, and I wondered why..."

"The wedding," he snorted. "I did that, too, used the old way, just to defy them. And they twisted it to serve their purpose, to invalidate the oath. They are clever, clever men. And now it provides an easy escape."

"For you. For them," I said. "Good soldiers always have their escapes clearly planned. How wonderful, to serve a purpose so lofty. Move forward quickly, keep your gaze on the figures in the clouds ahead, and you never need consider the flesh and bones you crush beneath your wheels."

Alfonso stood up. "I promised to acknowledge our children, and I will do so," he said hotly. "They will be raised as nobles, as children of the king—well-educated and well-married. They will not be set aside. Only you. And God knows I am sorry. I sinned against you, I am sinning against you still. You do not deserve this. The convent at San Pedro de las Dueñas is new and fine. It is the best I can do for you, Zaida."

He never before had called me by my name. He laid his cloak over his shoulders and kissed me lightly on the mouth. "Thank you," he said. "You still are a most beautiful woman."

And so he left. When the children returned I took them to my room and told them what I had learned. Much of it was shameful news to give children, but they were babies, bastards, too, by some peoples' lights. They would not remember any of it. It was treason for me to speak it, but I had to. I had to make myself believe it somehow.

By then was beyond worry. I hardened my heart against the past, and said goodbye to them, my precious daughters. I was prepared to give birth to the little one, and prepared to die.

24
I am Finished

There is a precision to my memories of the day that
followed. It was the most significant day of my life.

It began with a woman at my door whom I had never
seen before, a tall, pale woman with dirt in the folds of her
wrists and neck. She said she was a midwife, sent by the
king. I told her politely that I already had a midwife, and
her services were not needed. She went away. I returned to
my sewing.

She returned an hour later, this time with Sister Ana and
a monastery guard. The cook let them in, they crowded
into my little sitting room. No greetings were exchanged.
Sister Ana went straight to the point.

"Doña Isabel, the king has secured the services of the
best midwife in Leon, and you must cooperate," she told
me. "Your child will arrive very soon, no? You will need
her assistance. We can prepare the house, give you proper
food and care." The midwife handed a basket of vegetables
to the cook, and told her to stew them over a slow fire.

They would help bring on the labor, she said, and give me strength.

"A woman should not be alone at a time like this," Sister Ana said. The midwife nodded sagely.

"Sister Ana, I have been alone these many months, without occupying your mind for a moment's time," I said. "I have my own servants and my own midwife. At a time like this I do not intend to have strangers in my home. Please go now," I said.

Sister Ana drew herself up to her full height. "You are not the queen. You will do as the king orders," she said. "We cannot have a royal heir delivered by heathens."

"Sister Ana, you are an ignorant woman," I said. "Your people know nothing of bodies or medicine or even herbs. When the king orders me to have a farm-hand attend my birthing, I will do so, but for now I do not believe what you say. And I owe you no obedience."

"You soon will," she spat. Her face was red against her white wimple. "You will learn what obedience is. I promise you that. If you live."

"Go," I said. I opened the front door wide and stood beside it. They swept out into the street.

I closed the door and barred it. I could hear them outside, discussing in hot voices what they should do, then finally they went away. The cook and I cut up vegetables together, we put them in a pot to simmer with the last day's leftovers. I told her to go home. I sent the nurse and the little ones over to the convent. I needed to pray, I told them. I did not want the children in the house if things continued to go awry.

I sat down again by the fire. The weather was sharp and bright, a welcome break in the grey winter. The streets were full of shouting and chatter. The new queen was coming soon!

Almost noon, and a wagon stopped in the door yard. It was Olaya, sweating. She needed some things, she said—Caterina's baby was on its way. Could she take some of the herbs Yasmin had given me, maybe some bread? I gathered up all the herbs and food I could find in the kitchen, and the little pot of vegetables. She put the hot pot on the floor of the wagon, wrapped in clean rags, so it could stay hot and warm her feet, too She kissed my cheeks and told me to pray. The baby was coming fast.

Wait! I said, I want to come with you! I could ride inside the wagon unseen, without creating a scandal, and escape whatever scheme was going on with the new midwife. Perhaps I could help? I tucked my work-bag under my arm, threw on my cloak, locked up the house, and went with Olaya to the village at the bridge.

Something was wrong.

Women were gathered outside the sculptor's shack. The air smelled of blood. I sent in a little pomander of sweet-smelling cloves for Caterina to sniff or even chew—she loved scents. Don't go inside, the hermit said, come with me to the church. Come with me, he told the women round the door. Bring the children. Let's pray, he said.

I went with them into the sanctuary, four stone walls with timbers laid across the top to start the roof—only the altar was enclosed. A weak sun shone through the window-slits, and sparrows fluttered and argued. I played with the children. I read their fortunes in their palms. I braided the hair of the little girls. The people of the bridge knelt and prayed. Up at the altar was the sculpture—a placid woman with a smiling child on one arm, and a golden yellow apple in her other hand. Her dress was green over a yellow blouse, the same as I'd worn that shameful Sunday the year before. Her face was the image of Caterina's. I remembered I had the little Psalter in my work-bag. In a lull in the prayers I pulled it out and read a few verses aloud. The children gathered near to see the little pictures drawn into the margins, to touch the stiff pages.

Finally a weedy cry came from the dwelling, and a third boy was born to Caterina. Olaya and Yasmin scurried in and out the low door with cloths and bowls. The sculptor soon emerged to show us the tiny new creature. It was wrapped in rags, and looked with wise eyes past his father's face and into the blue sky. Lucas smiled wide, and the baby yowled! I stood to put the book away, and realized how thirsty I felt—I wanted water, lots of water. My heart raced, and I thought it was from excitement of the baby's arrival. Then I felt a tug inside me, and a gush of liquid heat below. It was my turn. When one baby cries, all the babies cry in sympathy. So it must be the same with being born.

Like Caterina's boy, mine also came on hard and fast. There was no time to go back to my house, or even to Hamid's. The hermit took me to his neat new room, perched me on a three-legged stool near the hearth, and loaded logs onto the fire. Olaya soon appeared, her hands shaking. The new baby was well, but Caterina had delivered with an excess of blood. Now she was ill, vomiting, losing consciousness. Strangely, Yasmin too was ill and vomiting.

I could not think. My body was overwhelmed with the work of birth. The baby came very quickly and easily, after only three hours or so, much like his eldest sister had done. Thank God for Olaya, who acted as midwife for me.

Just as the moon rose, just as the cavalcade of the new queen rolled past on the road outside, my son slipped into the murky light inside the hermitage at Our Lady of the Bridge. The hermit bundled him up in one of my under-skirts and anointed him with oil. Olaya helped me change out of my sweaty, spotted gown. Finally I curled up and slept with my baby in my arms, oblivious to the great activity going on around me. I think I never slept so well, before or since.

I awoke to hot bean broth and harried, haggard faces. Bright sunshine slid past the fabric hanging in the doorway. My boy slept on in the little bed in the straw... curled next to him, clinging against me, was a second baby. Tucked into his swaddling bands was the weird hairy charm that Caterina showed me in the cart all those years before, the little claw she wore round her neck. I felt a prickle down my back, and realized my head was uncovered. I felt for my coif, and felt a little bolt pass through me... my hair! My hair, my thick black braid—my braid was gone, crudely cut from my head! I felt the stubble with my fingers, felt my head, and a little wail escaped me. The hermit turned from his hearth and held up a hand to me.

"My hair!" I cried. The babies started, their blue eyes opened, their little cries joined mine. They looked identical at first, but I knew the firstborn, the one I'd seen before I fell asleep—he had a tiny dent in his chin, like Alfonso's. "Two babies!" I exclaimed.

"Yes, they both are boys. Now lie down, my lady!" the hermit cried, "Let me get Olaya, she will tell you what became of everything. Don't move from here, for the love of God!" He fled through the door.

My thoughts were confused, so I concentrated on matters at hand.

I arranged the babies at my breasts as well as I could, and felt that familiar surge of love flow through me as they took hold. They were swaddled tightly in the white bands I'd set aside for the purpose, back at my house. I smile still as I write! Quiet came down as they fed, and I felt myself grow peaceful.

Olaya came and helped me to dress. She was exhausted. "Zaida, forgive me, but I had to cut your hair," she said. "I took your prayer beads, too. We have had to work fast. We are scheming, to save you, to save the baby... the king's people were here in the night, they will come back soon, we have to work fast," she said.

When I was again presentable she called out the door, and Hamid, Esteban the hermit, and Lucas returned. Lucas' face was swollen with tears, and Pablito, one of his raggedy little boys clung to his tunic. Lucas took the smaller baby and held him tenderly in his lap. The little boy put out his finger, and the infant clutched it.

They sat round my pallet on the floor and told me what had happened in the night.

"The baby in Lucas' arms is his son," Hamid said. "We laid him beside you for your warmth, and to suckle, because his mother is dead," he said.

"Caterina is dead," Lucas said flatly. He squeezed the baby close. "What will we do now?"

"The pottage. The vegetables from your kitchen," Olaya said. "They tried to kill you, Zaida. Poison. They killed Caterina. The midwife is very sick. No one else ate the pottage. That was meant for you, the vegetable broth."

I was overwhelmed. I looked at poor Lucas, holding the tiny boy in his great arms, and I sobbed. I had brought nothing but sadness and loss to him.

"Lucas. I am sorry," I whispered.

"Women die in childbirth, lady," he said. "My own mother died bringing me to the world. My Caterina was prepared to die."

"And Caterina was the sacrificial lamb that makes a resurrection possible," the hermit said. "Her soul is even now in heaven, interceding for us. This will work, with her help." He patted the sculptor on the back, then turned to me. "My lady, we are presumptuous. We are undertaking a great treachery that could see us all killed within the next hours. We presumed to include you in our deception. We must tell you your part in this. You must forgive us."

"Your sin is my sin, then," I said, smiling. "Tell my what I've done."

"Zaida, the king's new bride is now at the monastery in San Facund. You left your house bolted and dark, so it was assumed you had fled—two of the guards came here in the night looking for you. Someone told them you were giving birth here. One rode back with the news. The other stayed to ensure the child was born alive. We fed him on the remains of the vegetable stew—he is suffering now down at the riverbank, but he won't die. They will be back at any moment to take the child. The prince. The bells have been ringing for an hour now."

I snuggled my baby near. "Oh dear God in heaven," I cried. My heart was breaking. My Sancha and Elvira—how I longed for them! I swallowed the knot of tears in my throat and tried to listen.

"We rode to your house when your pains began, and brought the swaddling, the bedding, your clothes. We brought your papers, your mule," Hamid said.

"We prayed together, the four of us," Esteban interrupted. "Olaya put your dress on Caterina's body. We washed her hands, and and wound her in your winding-sheet, and cut your braid to wind into the bandages, in the way of the Moors, with the tail exposed."

"Your rosary we lay inside as well. Your pomander already was clutched in her hand," Olaya said. She touched the baby's cheek.

"When they come for the prince, they will take away with them the body of his mother, now lying in the chapel," Hamid said. "We can only pray the king's men or the monks do not unwrap the body or inspect it too closely."

"They want Zaida dead. They expect it. This this will satisfy them," Olaya said. "The body of a woman dead in childbed, and a live baby boy. Now that they have their prince, they won't bother with the Moor."

My head swam, but I grabbed onto an idea. "My carpet, the yellow one. I sent it to your house," I said to Hamid. "Wrap Caterina in that, Hamid, please. If she is posing as a princess of Sevilla, she should be buried as a princess, if not a queen. Bind it on each end, like they do at home."

"So you are not appalled by our deception, Zaida?" Hamid asked. "I know how much you dislike lies."

"It is a lie devised to serve a greater truth," the hermit cut in. "Just see how all these things occurred together! Only the hand of God could achieve it! The king has his son. And you, good lady, have a chance to live."

"Yes. Thanks be to God. And to you. Where will I go?" I asked. "I have not considered what will happen next. I cannot go to that convent, and be a slave to that awful nun."

"Soon as the soldiers are gone you must go, straight away. You cannot stay here," Hamid said. "There are pilgrims here, good people, on their way north to see the relics of our Savior in Oviedo. I promised them the use of a cart and two good mules if they will take you with them, on a less-used route, to San Miguel de Escalada."

"The brothers will receive you there—bring them the Psalter," Esteban said. "You can tell anyone who asks that you are a pilgrim fulfilling a promise. I have written a letter for you to present to the abbot. He is a trustworthy man, and will advise you on where to go next."

"You can rest in the cart, recover your strength on the way," Olaya said. "Stay out of sight. Speak to no one. I have packed some things for you. There is tea in the green bag, be sure to take a cup morning and night, it will help the milk to dry... And food. And money, sewn into the sleeves of your red tunic. Hamid will bring the rest of your things to you, once you find a place. Send us word. Please, Zaida."

My baby opened his eyes and looked placidly into mine. I smiled at him.

"We will leave you for a moment with him, so you can say goodbye. I am sorry, lady," the hermit said. They filed out, and Hamid began shouting orders outside the door.

Olaya wept. The chapel the bell rang. My heart was full of joy and terrible pain, but I still did not cry.

"God keep you, little Sancho," I said. "You will be a great, wise, king. You will bring honor to Leon someday. And to Sevilla."

And so it was done. But for one last lie.

Outside the men were harnessing mules. Someone came for my things, to load them onto the wagon. Then Lucas slipped through the door, his babe in his arms. He came to where I sat and knelt beside us. He handed his baby to me, and took mine for a moment.

"Bless him, princess," he said quietly. "His name was to be Esteban, for the hermit. But I think it best if you christen him Sancho."

I took the tiny boy in my hands and kissed his forehead and thanked God and Our Lady for sending him to us. I prayed abundant blessings on him, and on the soul of his mother. I removed from around my neck the tiny golden cross I'd worn since my wedding day, and I put it over the baby's head.

And so the boy born to Lucas and Caterina became Prince Sancho of Leon. Moments later Olaya handed him over to Sister Ana and two monks of San Facund. They took him to live at the palace of the kings of Leon.

When I slipped from the hermit's hut into the mule-cart headed north, I held my own little boy in my arms.

25
FINAL WORDS

I have not written in many days. My vision is not good. I rejoice that my labor is almost finished. Here are some documents and letters, saved from the final days. They will tell the tale better than I could if I continued:

ANNOUNCEMENT to be read from EVERY PULPIT on the first Sunday before Lent

By order of Abbot Bernardo of San Facund and Metropolitan Archbishop of Toledo, prefect of parishes, monasteries, chapels, hermitages:

IN THE NAME OF CHRIST our LORD

REJOICING is in order this day, for on the 11th day of February in San Facund, Leon, was born a son, SANCHO, to our King Alfonso VI of Castilla, Leon, Galicia, Portugal, Toledo, Navarra, and Rioja.

No work shall be performed on this day, and a general feast is declared in the parishes, with sweetmeats, bread, cheese, and wine provided for all parishioners, pilgrims, mendicants, and monastics on the day of this announcement.

A PSALM shall be said at the end of the Mass of announcement, of optional attendance, for the repose of the soul of Doña Isabel of Denia, defunct of Alfonso the King, mother of the infant SANCHO, who was gathered unto the Lord in the discharge of her duties, interred this day in the chapel of the royals at the Monastery of San Facund.

THE LORD GIVETH; THE LORD TAKETH AWAY. BLESSED BE THE NAME OF THE LORD.

And here is a copy of a letter I left behind at San Miguel de Escalada some eight months later.

CUSTODIA

I, Isabel de Leon, do hereby give over to the holy brothers of San Miguel de Escalada authority and custody of my child Esteban de Leon, born in San Facund, for the term of two years, or until I return for him. For his support I leave a silver band set with gold leaves, wrought in Cordobes fashion, now crowning the image of Our Lady of Remedies in the parish church. Should I die or for other reasons not return after five years, I hand over full custody to the Brothers of San Miguel de Escalada, with the request that Estebanito be trained in the monastery workshop of the illuminators and sculptors; or if his talent so inclines him, in the choir of the monks.

Esteban de Leon is to be given full freedom at his 17th year, at which time he should be told the truth of his origins. A document to that effect is in the keeping of the prior. My son shall make his own decision as to his fitness for the cloister.

Isabel Denia de Leon
witnessed this day
San Miguel de Escalada
Kingdom of Leon

The next was written in Arabic. I translate it here:

Zaida, my friend:

I was so happy to hear from you at last, to simply know you are alive, and the child lives.

I will begin with happy news: I am father of a daughter named Zaida and a son named Brahim (or Elizabeth and Lucas, as you choose!) Another boy was given us, but he did not live through his first winter. Olaya is in fine health. I am a happy man.

The waterworks are functioning as planned, and the community of Our Lady of the Bridge thrives. I am now at work bringing the springs of San Facund to the street surface so each of the neighborhoods will have adequate water, and fewer accidents with deep-water and wells. Olaya sold the cattle yard two years ago. Her brother Ali has gone to the monks in Carrión, where his name now is Brother José. Our house is always full of children. The noise is endless.

We do not see the king among us these days. He is in the south and east, fighting. He is growing old, his beard is gone grey. He has got one child on the new queen, another daughter; his eldest daughter Urraca is mother to a son, so with young Prince Sancho, the succession is secure.

The prince is kept at court in Leon, no doubt in great splendor and comfort. I have not seen him since he was born, but I understand he is a healthy and strong, training in knightly pursuits.

Your daughters are gone these six months, off to be educated in the great city of Toledo. The women at the laundry pool say the nuns spoiled them terribly and fed them too much! Sancha is noted for her sweet singing voice, and Elvira for peevishness! A husband has been found for one of them, a prince of Sicily. Rejoice, my Zaida, for in Toledo the monks are not so strong, and there your girls may learn the poetry of their grandfather Mu´tamid as well as the Carolingian hand and the canticles of Our Lady and St. James the Apostle. There, I am told, our people live in peace, together with the Christians, Jews, and every kind of infidel. If it were not for my Olaya I would myself seek a life there—you know the archbishop himself has invited me!

But I am sure you wonder what became of our strange plot.

Princess, "your" body was laid in the tomb at San Mancio the same afternoon you left us, wrapped in the beautiful carpet as you commanded. The winding-sheets were not disturbed. You were sent off to heaven with a simple Mass and few hymns, and the king had a fine memorial stone placed over the spot, declaring you his much-beloved queen. The stone was moved over the tomb before the Mass began, and the hermit had a watch set up over the site, but somehow the monks managed to secure for themselves what they most desired. Your yellow Almeria rug now graces the abbot's private quarters. The old rascal robbed your grave.

The hermit Esteban is very old now, given to dreams and visions. One of the sons of the sculptor is taking Holy Orders soon, and will likely take his place at the chapel when the old man finally passes.

The people of Our Lady of the Bridge continue to pray for you by name each day at Nones. You are beloved here, Zaida.

You will find with this letter a folio of new poems, lately brought up from the south. I would not have sent them, but Olaya said it would hurt you more to remain in ignorance. This is the part so difficult to write, Zaida. With the arrival of the folio we learned what is become of our king, Mu´tamid ibn Abadid, and of your family.

The Almoravid Berbers swept across Al Andaluz in the past few years, pushing back the Christians and crushing the little Moorish kingdoms made so weak by fighting among themselves. Sevilla also fell, my princess. This cannot surprise you. Your brothers, alas, are gone, fallen in battles and rebellions. Your father, mother, and sisters are exiles now in the desert of north Africa. Your father continues to write from there, perhaps more beautifully than ever. His poems will tell you of their lives.

They strike me to my heart. To know I'tamid his noble wife was so ill when she heard of the death of her last son, to know his beautiful daughters—your sisters—are reduced to spinning wool to earn their bread. Ah, my heart breaks open! How I cry when I read the laments, to learn their ugly fate in such beautiful verse. Surely it would have been better for the king to die fighting than to be taken in chains to the river and sent away to the desert. To drift down the Guadalquivir past his gardens, his pleasure groves, his marble-paved orangeries, to leave them all in the hands of barbaric preachers!

Nowhere in the world is poetry to compare with that of Al-Mu'tamid. My children will know these verses, and their children, and they will know that their father and grandfather served the very poet in his palace when Sevilla was the jewel of the world, and Mu'tamid and I'timad the suns that gave it radiance.

With this letter comes the wagon with the possessions you left in our care, and a capital for your new chapel, a portrait in stone made by our friend Lucas of you, our princess, now a foundress of convents. I pray every blessing of Allah and of our Savior Christ upon you and your new life.

Perhaps someday we shall meet again.

There went a ruler from this pleasant spot,
Even Mu'tamid, mighty in his day;
And peradventure he returneth not,
But that which Allah wills shall none gainsay.

Hamid Ibn Khalikan
Jacob the Moor

Vanishing is a painful business, but it is liberating, too. I suffered at the monastery of San Facund, but I found a new life inside the walls of another religious house, a place humble and remote, far beyond the grasp of lofty Frenchmen. Now you have found my story there, too.

The riches that followed me from Sevilla likewise found me here in the craggy mountains. My Moorish silk and gold are turning to paving stones and roof timbers. Our little convent is growing, even though our novices are simple local girls. I teach them to read and write and to keep accounts using abacus and digits. We have flowing water, our rooms and bodies are clean and healthy. Our garden is beautiful. We do not often venture outside the walls. We keep the hours, sing our prayers, work and sleep and worship our Lord in perfect obscurity. No one from far away comes here to visit.

There is no reason to seek us out.

And so my story is told, my debts settled.

I am dead, and my life is hidden in Christ. I rest in peace.

EPILOGUE

Princess Zaida of Seville was a real person, but this story is a work of fiction, written from the scraps and stories that remain after almost 1,000 years.

History says Zaida Of Seville (born c. 1071) was a Muslim princess, mistress, and perhaps wife and queen of Alfonso VI of Castile. It is through her that many crowned heads of Europe trace their ancestry to the Prophet Muhammad.

Zaida, or Zayda, is said by Iberian Muslim sources to have been the daughter of Al Mu´tamid, the Muslim King of Seville, or perhaps his daughter-in-law.

She was forcibly converted from Islam to Christianity and taken to live in the north of what now is Spain. Records of her life there are contradictory and full of romantic legends. Some say she started a trend for Islamic arts, clothing, dance, and architecture in the courts of Leon and Burgos, and was deeply mourned when her short reign ended. Other chronicles say she was simply a concubine, mother to the bastard prince who was legitimized in order to be named the king's heir. Zaida/Isabel died in childbirth, but the date is unknown. It is unclear whether the child being delivered was Sancho, King Alfonso's only son.

She was buried in San Facund under the inscription, "H.R. Regina Elisabeth, uxor regis Adefonsi, filia Benabet Regis Sevillae, quae prius Zayda, fuit vocata." "Here lies Queen Isabel, wife of King Alfonso, daughter of Abenabeth, king of Seville; previously called Zaida."

The royal tombs were broken and desecrated in 1812, when Napoleon's troops passed through. Today, remains thought to belong to King Alfonso VI lie in a great stone sarcophagus in the chapel of the Madres Benedictinas convent. Across the apse, in a similar casket, are sealed the bones of four of his wives, including Zaida.

Zaida's daughters grew up and married well. Sancha married Rodrigo González, Duke of Lara; In 1117 Elvira married King Roger II of Sicily, a warrior and political player to equal her father. Theirs was a love match. They had six children together, and when the queen died her husband went into seclusion for so long it was rumored he was dead, too. (Some records, written later, say Elvira and Sancha were born to a different Queen Isabel, a French princess.)

Prince Sancho, heir to the throne of Castilla and Leon, was killed in the Battle of Uccles of 1108, during his father's lifetime.

When King Alfonso died, the throne went to his eldest daughter, the widow Urraca, daughter of Queen Constanza of Burgundy.

San Facund in the days of Zaida and Alfonso was on the rise, the center of Cluniac religious reform for the entire Iberian peninsula and a bustling market center on the

Camino de Santiago pilgrim trail. Its international popula-
tion and ethnic neighborhoods soon outgrew the city walls,
and when Muslim historian Idrisi visited in 1150 he found
"a well-populated, strong city of pleasing aspect and comfortable lodgings."

At its height the monastery of San Facund—the name
later contracted to Sahagún—controlled more than 90
other abbeys throughout Spain. Its university, scriptorium,
and library were famed for illuminated manuscripts, and
the vaulted dining hall was found "most magnificent and
worth seeing" by a 17th century Italian pilgrim. Eventually
the institution took up a large portion of the town, and
boasted four separate cloisters.

Its glory is now far away in the past.

The second half of the millennium saw Sahagún in steep
decline. The university moved to Navarre, the monastery was burned twice by the townspeople and again by
Napoleon's men. It fell into ruin when Spain's convents were
disestablished in 1835. A small community of Benedictine
nuns now resides in a corner of the once-massive monastic complex—their lives of quiet service are far from the
wicked fictions committed by the Benedictines in this tale!
They keep a small museum of antique art and finery, the
scraps left over from the monastery's glory days. A similarly
small and aging community of sisters sings the hours at San
Pedro de las Dueñas, 15 kilometers south of Sahagún.

Sahagún is a dusty market town, with low-rise apartment blocks, streets, and parks instead of cloisters and
scriptoria. The town of 12,000 souls now is home to fewer
than 2,800 people, but they maintain a lively sense of history. In 2009 they marked the millenium of King Alfonso

VI with costumed feasts, a home-grown opera, and elaborate dances in the park where the main cloister once stood. The pilgrimage to Santiago de Compostela revived in the 1990's after centuries of silence. The town is now, in the summer months, an important stopping-place for thousands of travelers from all over the world.

On the path into Sahagún, next to a little Roman bridge, pilgrims sometimes pause at the dark, tiny chapel of La Virgen del Puente, a jewel of the Sahagún Mudejar building style. Details of its foundation are lost to time.

After Zaida left Sevilla, Yusuf ibn Tashfin, the Almoravid Berber king, continued his dance of invasion and appeasement in the little Islamic states of Al-Andaluz. Zaida's father acted with valor on the field of battle, and folly in his political and diplomatic efforts. He tried to placate the Berbers by betraying to them his fellow Muslim princes, all while scheming with Alfonso against the Berbers. By 1091, Mu'tamid's time ran out, and the Almoravids stormed Seville. Mu'tamid fought bravely, but once surrounded he cut a deal, ordering his sons to surrender the fortresses they held in other cities. Mu'tamid, his wife and daughters were sent to exile in Africa, where some of his most moving poetry was written.

I wonder whether I ever shall spend another night
With flower gardens and water pools around me,
Where green olive groves, far famed, are planted,
Where the doves sing, the warbling of birds resounds.

When Abd Al-Jabbar, her last surviving son, was killed in battle in 1093, I'timad died of a broken heart. Her husband lived only another two years. Today, the red adobe tombs of Mu´tamid and I´timah are tourist attractions in the little Moroccan town of Aghmat, 33 kilometers from Marrakech. A simple stone column stands today in the gardens of the Alcazar in Sevilla, an apologetic tribute to the poet-king who was driven from his pleasure groves to a desert exile.

ABOUT THE AUTHOR

Rebekah Scott was a reporter and editor on American newspapers for 23 years. She now lives in a village of 21 people on the Camino de Santiago pilgrimage trail in northern Spain. In a former sheep-fold re-christened Peaceable Kingdom, she hosts pilgrims, raises animals, and writes novels based on the colorful stories she finds everywhere around her. "Big Fun In A Tiny Pueblo," her popular blog, details her ongoing adventures.